The SONG of the SWAN

ALSO BY KARAH SUTTON

A Wolf for a Spell

The
SONG of the
SWAN

Karah Sutton
illustrations by Pauliina Hannuniemi

Alfred A. Knopf
New York

THIS IS A BORZOI BOOK PUBLISHED BY ALFRED A. KNOPF

Visit us on the Web! rhcbooks.com

Educators and librarians, for a variety of teaching tools,
visit us at RHTeachersLibrarians.com

Library of Congress Cataloging-in-Publication Data is available upon request.
ISBN 978-0-593-12169-6 (trade) — ISBN 978-0-593-12170-2 (lib. bdg.) —
ISBN 978-0-593-12171-9 (ebook)

The text of this book is set in 11.25-point Horley Old Style MT Pro.
The illustrations were created using Adobe Photoshop and
self-made paper and watercolor textures.
Editor: Katherine Harrison
Cover Designer: Bob Bianchini
Interior Designer: Jen Valero
Copyeditors: Artie Bennett and Alison Kolani
Managing Editor: Jake Eldred
Production Manager: Nathan Kinney

Printed in the United States of America
10 9 8 7 6 5 4 3 2 1
First Edition

Thank you, Dad,
for encouraging my voice,
whether in writing or song

"Gather round," said the old spider.
The little ones drew close,
for he was a great spinner of stories.

The SONG of the SWAN

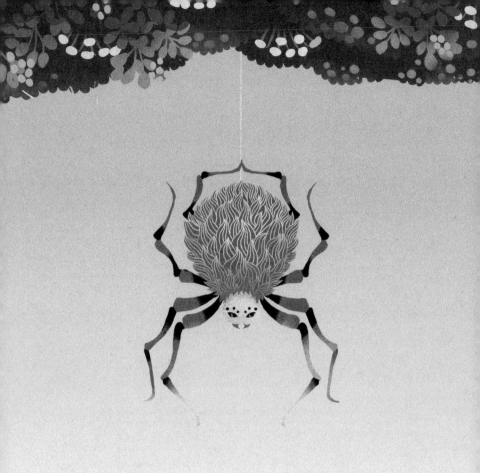

The Spider Spins
His First Tale

You may have heard, little ones, a story or two about the secrets of the human heart. You must already know that hearts possess powerful magic. But did you know that it was a spider who gifted this magic to humans? Yes! It is true! Let me tell you the tale.

Long ago, a young human from this very valley had to leave his home and venture out into the world for the first time. His heart ached at the thought of leaving his parents and grandparents behind. He would miss his valley's shimmering lake and the white birch trees gracing its hills. The sound of his father's laughter. The smell of his grandmother's freshly baked bread.

In those days the valley was protected by a great spider queen, and the young man approached her for guidance and wisdom.

"Spider queen," he said with a respectful bow, "soon I must leave my family behind and enter the wider world. But I fear leaving them will break my heart in two."

The spider queen was very old and very wise, and she considered his concerns awhile. She tapped a spindly leg against her tree-root throne as she pondered. Soon an idea came, one that would allay this young man's fears.

She withdrew a strand of her own silk and used her spider magic to carefully wrap it around his heart. The end of the strand coiled at his chest to form a faint silver circle barely visible to his human eye. The opposite end she tied to a tree root. As she released it, the strand shimmered in the sunlight before becoming invisible. No one but this young man would see or feel its presence.

"With my gift," she said, "you will hold this valley in your heart and you will forever be connected to it." But the spider queen was very generous, and she couldn't help herself—she could see the young man's goodness, and she desired to let him in on a secret. "The string will bring you strength that you cannot imagine, for you are now tied to the energy of the earth. It is a power that has never been wielded by humans. Yet its use carries risk, even danger. Do you still desire this boon?"

It is regrettable that her keen eyes could not see into the future or she might not have given this power so readily.

The young man accepted her gift, and as he traveled far and wide, he held his home in his heart. The spider's string gave him what humans have come to call "magic," but he never used it, even after returning to the valley years later. In time he forgot the strand's promised powers.

Though his string remained invisible and untouched, his children were born with these "heartstrings," and their children too. Soon the strands spread to those who were not his relations, and after a great many years, every person in the tsardom had a heartstring hidden inside them.

The power of these heartstrings was not altogether lost. Every so often, a child was born with the ability to see and wield the strand's magic.

But forgotten was the spider queen's warning. Magic had power, but its use could bring pain and suffering. A long time later, suffering did ensue, and a dark shadow would fall over this valley. Though this shadow fell after his lifetime, it was a curse that almost destroyed the young man's beloved home.

So I ask you, little ones: the young man got his wish, but was it worth the price?

one

Years of traveling with a notorious swindler had taught Olga an important lesson: people who are trusting are the easiest to trick.

So she ignored the obvious lies being spun by her deceitful guardian as she jabbed her needle into the sewing in her lap.

"My illustrious lady!" shouted Mr. Bulgakov at a passing woman. "Don't be shy. Your beauty needs no decoration, but our fine jewelry will complement the sparkle of your eyes."

Mr. Bulgakov gave his usual speeches to the visitors of the market, but so far no one had been drawn in. Other merchants were beginning to disassemble their stalls, and very few stragglers meandered past, those who did only half listening to Mr. Bulgakov's entreaties. "Jewelry, fine fabric, delicate trinkets, and music boxes! We have sold to tsars and kings and sultans, so exquisite are our wares!"

Behind the wagon, Olga stayed hidden. She wasn't good at interacting with customers. She yanked the thread, groaning as she made yet another messy stitch that her magic could not quite hide.

There was a rustle of fabric, and Mr. Bulgakov peeked around the tent to glare at her. "This is your fault. They can see through your magic—they know that the merchandise is shoddy." His cheeks were red beneath his beard from the heat of the day. Dust from the road flecked the brim of his cap.

Olga bit back the temptation to tell him that he could lie a little less extravagantly, but that was a criticism he would not receive well. And his critique of her magic was accurate— her crudely knotted heartstring around the tin necklaces and threadbare fabrics could fool only one person in ten. Most people could discern that something wasn't right, even if they couldn't tell that magic was involved.

"Psst, Olga, what do you think?"

She turned to find Pavel admiring himself in a mirror at the stall next to theirs, sporting an embroidered tunic and outrageous hat. The tunic looked well made, and the fabric hung elegantly on Pavel's hulking form, but: "The hat's too small for your big head," she hissed.

"You're right," Pavel whispered, swapping out the first hat for another, this time with a ridiculous feather.

"That's a ladies' hat," she said, trying to focus on her own stitching.

"I still think it suits me," said Pavel. He turned back to the mirror and stroked the feather on this new hat, flicking his bushy red eyebrows up and down and wrinkling his nose. He was nearly eighteen, a good five years older than Olga, but sometimes he acted like a younger brother.

Her stomach rumbled. She would need to learn how to prepare better illusions if she wanted to avoid going hungry so often. The meager stash of coins from their last sale was already running low.

Mr. Bulgakov claimed that one day their trickery would yield a sum so grand that they would never go hungry again, but in the meantime a life of swindling was their only choice.

And now he would demand that Olga steal food, since they hadn't managed to sell anything at the market.

Olga looked once more at her embroidery, wishing the knobby birds and malformed roses were beautiful enough that she could sell her work without resorting to illusion. She gave Pavel a sidelong glance. "Looks like I'll need to find some supper for the evening."

Pavel returned the hat and cloak and ducked behind their wagon beside Olga. His long legs knocked over boxes of wares, which scattered, making a loud enough racket to drown the sound of Mr. Bulgakov's voice. Pavel gave the old man a smile and stooped to set everything right again with a quick "Sorry!" Poor Pavel was always forgetting how tall he was.

"Don't bother," said Mr. Bulgakov. "We might as well pack everything away anyway. Olga, find us some food before it's all gone—"

"I'm going, I'm going," Olga muttered. She was already a few paces away from their wagon, venturing out into the half-shuttered market.

With practiced fingers, Olga swiped what she could from the final few stalls: old potatoes, a couple of apples. She reached to her chest and withdrew a short length of her heartstring—the magic glimmering in a way that only she could see—and used it to lasso a bit of cheese off a table and into her waiting hand.

When she returned to their wagon, Mr. Bulgakov wrinkled his nose.

"That's the best you could do?" he said. "That won't last us one meal, let alone to the next village."

Olga bristled. She hated it when Mr. Bulgakov made her feel like a disappointment. "What would you have done?" she snapped.

"That stall is selling meat pies," he said, gesturing to a table balanced at the end of a rickety cart. "Bring us one of those."

Olga took a step toward the stall, then hesitated. At the front of the stall, two children younger than her were playing a chasing game of some sort. They giggled and shrieked with laughter. Their shoeless feet slipped on loose stones, and their clothes had bare patches and threads unraveling at the hems. It was one thing to swindle people who could afford the fake jewelry they sold, or to steal an apple that was no better than pig food, but stealing a whole pie from a struggling family felt different.

Sensing her reluctance, Mr. Bulgakov waved the young children over. "You there! Do you want to see something *wondrous?*" he said.

The boy, who looked to be the older of the two, stopped chasing his sister when Mr. Bulgakov called. The sister ducked behind him, peering under her brother's arm at the strangers. Mr. Bulgakov had timed his greeting well: The parents were in the midst of packing away their cart and had disappeared behind it. There was no one to usher the children away.

"I see you have a few pies remaining," Mr. Bulgakov observed, confident that the children were still listening. "We can trade."

Olga was about to ask what on earth he planned to tempt these children with when he reached under their cart to withdraw a small music box.

A sharp laugh nearly choked her. The music box ruse was a trick to swindle wealthy aristocrats with more money than sense. Olga would use her magic to craft an illusion that the figure inside the box could move on its own, like a puppet without strings. But these kids were from a working family, the kind that prized every loaf baked, every pail of milk from their goats. The cracked boards on the family's cart and the thread-bare patches on their clothes made this obvious. What on earth would they do with a music box?

Still, the children crept close, and Mr. Bulgakov gave Olga a meaningful look as he opened the music box, leaning forward so that the little girl was afforded a clear view of the sculpted dancer spinning inside.

When Olga didn't move, Mr. Bulgakov gave her a sharp jab with his elbow, then cleared his throat.

Olga's insides twisted. The elbow meant that he wanted her to perform magic. She could bewitch the box to make it something these kids couldn't refuse, and they were unlikely to see through her illusions. But the thought made unease bubble inside her.

"These are usually sold for a silver coin," Mr. Bulgakov said to the children, pausing to let the boy's eyes light up at the mention of so much money. "You could sell this at the next market and get much more for it, I am certain."

Beside her, Pavel tensed. "I thought we only took from people what they can stand to lose," he said in a low whisper.

"We take from people whose need is less than ours! They are not starving!" Mr. Bulgakov snapped in a voice pitched so only Olga and Pavel could hear. To Olga's surprise, his expression shifted to one of pleading.

Olga closed her eyes, wanting to ignore him, to walk away from these children and their remaining pies. But she didn't.

After her mother's death, Olga had tried to find out about

her father but been able to learn nothing other than that he was born somewhere in the Kamen Mountains. With no other relatives to care for her, Olga needed Mr. Bulgakov's reliance on her magic to give her a home. Even if that home was only the cart they used to get from village to village.

So she tugged a small strand of magic from her chest and reached out to take the music box from Mr. Bulgakov, acting as though she intended to demonstrate how it worked. With shaking fingers, she looped the strand of magic around the dancer, wrapping the tiny sculpture in an illusion that made her dance more lifelike than any wooden carving could be. The eyes of the children widened in wonder as they watched the dancer twist and twirl, finishing at last with a low curtsy.

The girl was itching to touch it. She'd emerged from behind her brother, her fingers twitching. She bit her lip. Her brother reached down and gave her hand a squeeze,

then nodded, smiling. The girl squealed with glee, then in a burst of speed turned and ran back to their cart, returning a moment later with a pie on outstretched hands. She nearly tripped in her haste, her bare feet managing to quickly recover on the uneven cobbles, and she clutched the pie close as a newly hatched duckling.

Wordlessly she offered the pie to Mr. Bulgakov before reaching eagerly for the music box. Olga hesitated but finally placed it in her tiny hands.

Olga turned away guiltily, refusing to see the delight on their young faces. In an instant, Mr. Bulgakov had hidden the pie within the cart and begun dismantling the remainder of their market display.

"Time to be on our way," he said, "quickly! Before those parents notice it's gone!"

Olga began moving items and crates back into the cart, but Pavel was nowhere to be seen. "Pavel?"

Where was he? Olga turned and saw him standing near the children's cart. The parents were still out of view as they packed away their remaining items. He slipped his hand toward the table where the pies had been, and Olga thought she saw the glint of a coin placed there, left behind for the family to find.

Before Mr. Bulgakov could even notice Pavel missing, the young man had returned, lifting two boxes at a time into their own cart.

Olga's stomach rumbled again, and she withdrew one of the apples she'd taken and took a bite. It was floury, but it was food, and she managed to chew a little instead of swallowing as quickly as she could.

But a voice from behind her made her blood run cold.

"There, Magistrate Morozova, Your Honor. That's the girl who stole from me."

Olga turned, her hand still clutching the apple, and saw a tall woman wearing a seal and badge that identified her as a regional magistrate. Beside her was an older man who Olga recognized from the apple cart. The magistrate's eyes narrowed as the man's finger pointed toward Olga.

The magistrate rested a hand on the hilt of her sheathed sword, a silent message to Olga not to attempt to run away. "I've had several reports of food stolen by a trio whose members include a girl and a giant young man with flaming hair," she said with a nod to Pavel's incriminating mane. "Care to explain?"

two

Nearby, Pavel stiffened. Olga could sense his fingers twitching, wanting to reach for a weapon. He was the protector, the one large enough and strong enough to fight if they needed him to. But they weren't in an alley, or a pub, or a darkened room. And this magistrate was armed—a sword glinted at her hip, and she was likely carrying other concealed weapons. A dagger in her boot, perhaps even a pistol. If Pavel fought, there was a chance he could get seriously hurt.

How much magic did Olga have left? She'd already used so much. If she used more than she could spare, there was a chance she would wind up unconscious on the ground.

But that was a risk she'd have to take.

She moved her hand just a hair, slowly and cautiously enough to avoid the notice of the magistrate. Her fingers brushed the warm coil of magic at her heart. Its familiar hum tingled against her fingers, dancing and shimmering with power. With a pinch and a tug, she twirled the end around her finger until she had enough to span the distance between them. It unfurled from her chest, a cobra performing its hypnotic dance.

A slow breath, then a snap as she whipped it through the air separating her and Pavel from the magistrate and the merchant. The illusion of dense fog bloomed, growing large enough to swallow their cart and the surrounding stalls, dense enough to confuse any onlookers and hide their escape.

In an instant, Olga could feel the effects of using more magic than she ought. Her knees weakened, threatening to give way, and her eyes started to roll back into her head. Pavel moved to catch her before she collapsed, throwing her over his shoulder as though she were nothing but a sack of potatoes. A sense of safety washed over her. Mr. Bulgakov might race to protect himself, but Pavel would never leave her behind.

Olga had managed not to faint completely, and she was awake enough to feel Pavel throw her into the back of the cart as he shouted "Go!" to Mr. Bulgakov, and to feel the lurch as Mr. Bulgakov flicked the reins and spurred their overworked horse, Fabiy, into action.

Olga released a breath of relief, but she was too quick. The neighing of horses and the stamping of hooves sliced the air as villagers gave chase.

"Be wary!" a gruff voice shouted. "They have a heartstringer with them!"

Oh no. She should have known that revealing her magic would make these people even more determined to catch them.

The cart jostled over the bumpy road through the village, then turned sharply as Mr. Bulgakov steered them onto one of the roads leading out of town in the direction of the mountains.

"Not much farther till the forest!" he shouted. "Just hold them off till we get there!"

For a second Olga tried to sit up. She reached a shaky hand toward her chest, even though she was too dizzy to see what was right in front of her.

A hand grabbed her wrist, and Pavel said sternly, "Don't you dare," before he let go again. She heard the thwack of his crossbow releasing a bolt and knew that Pavel had this under control.

Hoping she hadn't doomed them all to a future stay in a less-than-luxurious jail cell, Olga passed out then and there in the cart, the overuse of magic overtaking her at last.

Olga woke to the gentle sway of the cart and the patter of Fabiy's hooves. Only the gnawing in her stomach gave any indication of how much time had passed.

Pavel was sitting beside her, watching her wake.

"How are the blini?" he said.

Olga grinned. It was a joke they shared. Blini were her favorite pancakes, especially when they were smothered in stewed berries. But it had become a sort of code between them to say "blini" whenever she'd overused her magic. It had started as "wobbly knees"—always the first symptom—and then that

became "wah-blinis" and finally simply "blini." No one else knew what they meant, and Olga was glad that they could speak of it without revealing her magic. You never knew how people might react.

She placed a hand on her chest, feeling for that tremble of magic. When she used too much, her heartstring withered like an overly pruned shrub. But given enough sleep, it grew back. It seemed to be mostly restored now.

"Fine. Never better," she answered.

Pavel patted her on the shoulder. "There's water just there"—he pointed to the waterskin near her head.

Olga took a grateful sip. "How long has it been?" The cover had been assembled over the back of the cart, sheltering Olga and Pavel inside.

"Hours. It's nighttime. We're in the Kamen Mountains now."

Mr. Bulgakov didn't like driving after sunset if he could help it. Olga lifted the flap of the cart to peek outside. They were in a dense forest, the trees close enough on all sides to make it difficult to see more than a few feet. A sharp wind blew, and the air was thick with fog. Such fog was unusual in summer, and Olga peered around her, trying to make out the direction of the road.

Together she and Pavel climbed toward the front of the cart, slipping through a slit in the fabric to sit next to Mr. Bulgakov on the driving bench.

Mr. Bulgakov's face was wrinkled with concentration. He watched the road through narrowed eyes, flicking the reins to urge Fabiy onward at a brisk pace.

"I'm sorry about the villagers," said Olga, assuming that the chase out of the village was the reason they hadn't yet stopped to make camp.

"Huh?" said Mr. Bulgakov, blinking. Then he shook his head. "Oh, no, we've escaped worse. But I got turned around in these mountains."

A moaning wind seemed to respond to his words. Olga shivered, though she stopped herself before Mr. Bulgakov or Pavel saw. Beside her, Pavel had pulled out his domra and was plucking the strings of the instrument and singing to himself, *"The moon opens bright eyes, then she peers down and sighs. . . ."* Olga knew the folk song well, but it sounded more sinister on a night like this when they couldn't see their surroundings through the fog.

Above them something screeched. Fabiy stamped his hooves, looking as uneasy as Olga felt. Even Mr. Bulgakov was pale beneath his beard.

"Why haven't we made camp yet?" she asked.

Mr. Bulgakov kept his eyes on the road. "People tend to get lost around here. I want to get us back on the main road before stopping for the night."

As he said this, the road curved and the fog parted to reveal a moonlit sky. A valley stretched out before them. Steep hills sloped away toward a lush forest broken up by ravines slicing into the mountainside. At the bottom, the trees gave way to an enormous lake gleaming in the pale light.

"Where are we?" Olga asked.

Mr. Bulgakov sucked in a breath, as if realizing something. "The Sokolov Palace used to be in the valley."

"Used to be?"

"No one lives there now. No one goes looking either."

The name tugged at some memory in her mind. They'd driven a little farther around the rim of the valley, keeping that glittering lake in sight, when she remembered why she'd heard of the Sokolov Palace. It was rumored to house a rare stone, the Scarlet Heart.

The stone was said to be a jewel so beautiful that it was the envy of the tsar himself. Olga had never heard more than that, but she'd always imagined a blood-red ruby the size of her fist, cut in a heart shape that caught the light and made the gem glow as if aflame.

Olga's throat tightened. *So near.* They were only a few hours' ride from a treasure the likes of which they'd never encountered—and likely never would again.

As if sensing her excitement, Mr. Bulgakov nudged Fabiy faster, and they followed the turn of the road away from the valley's rim. Olga couldn't help but look behind them with longing. She thought of all the times Mr. Bulgakov had reminded them to look after themselves. She'd traveled with him, allowed him to train her in sleight of hand and pickpocketing. They'd raided carriages, plucked eggs from henhouses, approached lush manor homes and pretended to be respectable servants in order to nick trinkets and disappear during the night.

She'd always told herself that she didn't have a choice other than stealing and swindling. She could either use her magic as Mr. Bulgakov ordered her to do or find someone else who would take in an orphan like her, feed her, and clothe her, as

Mr. Bulgakov did. She didn't have many options, and in the end, she had to look after herself.

Suddenly it felt like another option had presented itself. If they could obtain the jewel, it would be enough to end all worries. Perhaps even the tsar would reward them for finding the lost object he coveted. They'd never want for anything when they possessed something so valuable.

"Don't even think about it," said Mr. Bulgakov, and it took Olga a moment to snap her eyes away from the road and to realize that Mr. Bulgakov had clearly guessed the direction of her thoughts. The moonlight made him look older and more tired than she'd seen him before. His scruffy beard was threaded with gray, and lines had formed about his nose and eyes.

Olga thought for a moment about pretending that she didn't know what he was talking about, but he knew her too well. "Why not?" she said.

But he didn't answer. They drove deeper into the mountains. At last Mr. Bulgakov slowed Fabiy's trot, and he steered the cart to a thicket set away from the road. Pavel leapt from his seat to gather firewood, and soon the scent of the savory pie they'd taken made Olga's mouth water as it warmed on a stone near the flames.

Her stomach clenched, and she remembered the jewel, still within walking distance down the road. If she could find it, they would never have to experience hunger. Never have to trick toiling families.

As Mr. Bulgakov handed her a slice of the pie, Olga seated herself by the fire and repeated her question. "Why can't we go after the jewel?" she asked. "There aren't any stories of someone else finding it. It must still be hidden in that valley somewhere."

"Because you'll never make it out of those woods," Mr. Bulgakov said through a mouthful of pie. He swallowed. Steam puffed from his mouth. "They'll kill you before you get to the palace."

This wasn't at all what Olga was expecting. Who would kill her? "Bandits?" she asked. "Pavel could take them."

"Take them where?" asked Pavel, dreamily staring skyward.

Olga gave him a pat on the shoulder but didn't answer.

Mr. Bulgakov ignored him. "Demons, monsters," said the older man. His voice had taken on a rasping, serious tone. "That valley is haunted." The firelight glowed against his cheeks and cast deep shadows over his eyes, giving him the look of some mysterious forest spirit.

Oh. Olga held back a laugh.

She knew there were things to be afraid of. And she knew there were unexplainable things she didn't understand. But she was pretty sure that monsters weren't one of them. This sounded like another one of Mr. Bulgakov's stories, the kind he and Pavel enjoyed sharing by firelight, much to Olga's annoyance.

But Mr. Bulgakov wasn't finished. "It's said that the valley contains a dark force with an endless hunger. Some years ago, everyone in the palace went missing. Now there is no one but that hungry specter, guarding the cursed jewel."

Olga avoided his gaze, instead staring at Fabiy grazing near their campfire. The horse's ears flicked in agitation. Something about the valley, that lake, made her itch. As if begging her to come investigate. As if she could feel strands of magic hovering and humming in the air, trailing back down the road the way they'd come. For a moment she thought she envisioned a single thrumming strand. She wanted to follow it to its end, wherever that led.

"Surely you don't believe any of that," she said. "It's all just stories."

"Some things are real when it seems like they aren't, and some things aren't real when it seems like they are. But that place? I believe the stories. No jewel could tempt me down there."

Disappointment crept into Olga's throat. This was a chance at a new and different life. Why should they hold back?

Mr. Bulgakov tilted his head to look at her. "What would you do with untold riches, Olga?" he asked. The question seemed teasing, but there was a seriousness to his tone. "Buy a palace?"

The question made Olga pause. The truth was, she didn't know what she would do with any treasure she managed to find—all she knew was what she could stop doing. She could stop going to sleep hungry. She wouldn't keep having to choose between stealing and having nothing. She could stop traveling if she wished. Or travel more. Maybe that was the true burden of her situation now—it felt like she'd never had a choice. It was that choice which she wanted most.

He sighed. "If you're looking to escape this existence of ours, beware: *that* hope is an illusion." He licked the last of the pie from his fingers and slipped into his bedroll, turning so that his back was to her.

Olga wanted to reply but couldn't find the words. A couple of minutes passed, and soon Mr. Bulgakov's snores filled the clearing. Pavel had fallen asleep too, his back against a rock, his instrument still in his lap. Olga tiptoed close and took it from him, placing it gently beside him. Then she draped Pavel's blanket over his shoulders.

She needed sleep too. She was supposed to rest after overusing her magic. But she lay in her own bedroll, her eyes refusing to close, her heart thumping loudly enough to pulse in her ears. Mr. Bulgakov's warnings about the valley were like a thorn in her palm. What he'd said couldn't be true. He was the one who'd promised that one day they would find a way to escape this life on the road, always hungry, always tired and anxious. Had he lied?

Suddenly an anger filled her, simmering with the poisonous sting of betrayal. For so long, she had tried to be grateful that Mr. Bulgakov had given her something resembling a family and a home. But a small part of her had always known that he was just using her. Her magic made it easy for him to swindle people. He didn't care about her, or Pavel either. Pavel was just the protector, the guard. And now, when there was a chance that they could improve things for good, Mr. Bulgakov was tying them down.

He needed her more than she needed him.

A plan had begun to form in her mind. It felt rash, even dangerous. But it was a chance worth taking.

three

"I have an idea," Olga whispered in Pavel's ear. It was still the middle of the night, though a few hours had passed, during which Olga had tossed and turned, waiting for the right moment. If she didn't act now, they would miss their chance.

Unsurprisingly, Pavel didn't move. He hadn't moved after she shook his shoulder either. Or poked him with a stick. The trick would be finding a way to wake him without waking Mr. Bulgakov too.

She took a piece of grass and tickled his nose. He swatted at it, and his eyes flickered.

Nearly there.

More tickling. This time Olga whispered, "There's a spider on your face."

In an instant, Pavel slapped at his nose and sat up straight. The blanket tumbled from around his shoulders. He grabbed his domra as if he planned to bludgeon someone with it.

"*Shhh!*"

Pavel blinked, finally noticing that Olga was crouched beside him. "What's going on?" he asked.

"I have an idea," Olga repeated. "An idea that could change our lives."

Pavel looked at her expectantly.

"Come with me to find the Scarlet Heart."

There was silence while the words wriggled through Pavel's sleep-addled brain. He blinked again. At last, he shrugged. "Okay."

Good old Pavel. Willing to go along with anything. And if he hadn't heard Mr. Bulgakov's speech about the hungry spirit, then he didn't need to know.

Olga certainly wasn't worried. She hardly ever believed in stories. People liked to tell them because they were fun, or thrilling, or comforting, not because they were true. And this story sounded like it had more embellishments than a rich man's coat.

They each kept a satchel for storing their personal belongings, so in the work of a moment they were packed to leave, and soon they stood at the edge of their camp, watching the rise and fall of Mr. Bulgakov's chest as he slept. Pavel gripped the staff he used as a weapon with one hand and his domra with the other.

"Are you sure you want to come with me?" Olga whispered. "It might be dangerous."

"If it might be dangerous, that's all the more reason why I should come with you," Pavel replied.

Olga felt a pang of guilt at sneaking away like this, but it was quickly overtaken by the excitement of the planned heist. They were about to embark on an adventure, and it was hard to devote attention to what they were leaving behind. Pavel laid an arm around her shoulder, and the warmth was comforting as they faced the dark unknown.

With a final nod of thanks for looking after her, Olga bade Mr. Bulgakov a silent goodbye, and together she and Pavel moved away from the dim glow of dying embers.

Clouds had obscured the moon. They followed the road through thick shadows, hesitant to make any noise or call attention to themselves until they were well out of sight of the camp. Owls hooted overhead. Somewhere in the mountains was the distant rumble of a waterfall.

When they'd walked nearly an hour in silence, Olga breathed a sigh, taking heart that Mr. Bulgakov had not woken and followed them. This was a good start. Carefully, so as not to use too much magic, Olga withdrew a small length of heartstring and let it glow to light the path ahead.

She found it calming to walk in silence alongside Pavel, her few belongings jangling in the satchel on her back. Pavel plucked at the strings of his domra as they gained distance from the camp. Another two hours had passed before the road turned and that now-familiar view of the valley stretched out before them. An itch prickled the back of Olga's neck. The sky had begun to lighten to a deep blue; the lake below lay still and gray.

Where the road turned, an abandoned cart blocked the path. Its wheels were missing, and nails had been pulled from the splintered boards. They slipped around it, but Olga's eye caught on some markings scratched into the wood.

TURN BACK

Her lip twitched at the ominous warning. The words had likely been carved by someone whose imagination matched Mr. Bulgakov's.

Pavel was ahead of her on the path. He mustn't have noticed the markings, or at least hadn't stopped to read them. She decided she wouldn't call his attention to them.

The road forked, and the left path veered down into the valley. Pavel paused. He looked at Olga, waiting for her to take the first step.

"Ready?" she asked.

He nodded.

Together they crossed an invisible threshold and began their descent.

In Olga's experience, forests were usually full of activity—particularly just before dawn, when the birds began their morning chorus—but in this forest she heard only the snapping of twigs beneath their feet.

The sky paled and the shadows shifted as the trees glowed pink under the rising sun. It was clear that this path wasn't used often—it was overgrown with ferns and littered with fallen tree branches. At times it disappeared entirely. Pavel was adept at navigating difficult terrain, so he took the lead and Olga followed him closely as the path cut switchbacks across the steepest slopes.

It would take at least until midday to reach their destination. But that would give them the whole afternoon to search the empty palace, and Olga had already begun plotting the most efficient ways to check room by room. She counted the turns of the path, each one bringing them closer to their goal. One, two . . . fifteen, sixteen . . .

Pavel hummed and played his domra as they walked. And as usual, he forced Olga to sing with him. He'd spent years trying to teach her how to play as well, but that was a step too far. When he insisted, she would sing, but no more than that.

"On a road dry with dust,
On a harsh mountain peak,
No matter which way we might roam,
Wherever you are, I am home."

She'd never told Pavel that her heart ached every time she sang, because singing brought back the few memories she had of her mother.

Olga's mother used to sing to herself as she stirred their porridge. The voice was husky and rough, concealing an inner softness. When a sad song about a dying bird had made Olga cry, her mother held her close and shed tears alongside her. Then when the tears had dried, they mixed extra berries into the porridge and savored the sweetness. Olga could still see the marks of dried tears over freckles dusting her mother's nose and glistening in her auburn lashes.

Her mother had been too tired to sing after sickness came to their one-room home. And at only six years old, Olga was too choked with emotion to sing at her mother's humble funeral.

But no, those were old memories, and Olga tried not to think on them. If she allowed herself to show any sadness, it was just another reason for Mr. Bulgakov to criticize her. He always said that sniveling distracted from their work.

And he was right. Tears were a weakness, she thought.

So she pushed the thoughts into a shadowy corner of her mind and focused on the moment in front of her. She was no good at singing and didn't much care for the song itself, but she added her voice to Pavel's anyway.

"Down a well or a mine,
Down a river or creek,
Wherever you are, I am home.
Together we're never alone."

Finally, he spoke aloud. "Do you really think there's a monster in this valley?"

Olga grunted. "I think Mr. Bulgakov tells lots of stories."

"Do you think we could get lost?" he said. He didn't seem frightened, simply wondering, as if he were asking whether she thought it was going to rain.

"I won't let that happen to us."

Pavel thought on this for a moment. "But sometimes," he said, "sometimes bad things happen even when people are trying to avoid them. No matter how careful they are."

"We won't get lost," she said, hoping that put an end to the matter.

"We could."

"Thanks for the optimism," she said, failing now to hide her annoyance. "If we got lost, we'd just find our way out again."

He was either satisfied with her answer or had sensed her irritation, because he returned to plucking at his domra and singing a low tune.

Streams gushed past them in short waterfalls. Slick stones tumbled out from under their feet. Olga had to clutch at Pavel to steady herself. The farther they went, the more the woods seemed to close in around them. Stout trees crowded close to the path. The white bark of birches gave the persistent impression of figures in pale cloaks lurking nearby.

They'd been walking for more than six hours since leaving camp when the lack of sleep caught up with the travelers and they stopped for a moment to rest. Without meaning to, Olga closed her eyes. She must have dozed, because she woke with a sudden jolt.

OooEEEaaaooo. Olga sat up, certain she'd heard the moan of a creature in distress, but the sound was gone. She shook her head. Of course she hadn't heard anything—the stories of monsters were nothing more than tales meant to frighten and thrill.

"You didn't hear anything, did you?" Olga asked.

"You were snoring a little?" said Pavel.

Olga swatted at him but didn't ask further questions.

Olga was annoyed to realize that her nap had cost them several hours. It was past midday, and the base of the valley was still well below them, when the trees parted enough for Olga to assess the view. She picked up her pace, moving ahead of Pavel to lead them along the path.

They continued until a cloud shifted, obscuring the sun. Pavel slowed, choosing his footsteps more carefully, calling to Olga to slow down. They'd traveled through many forests with Mr. Bulgakov, and Pavel had never been frightened of animals or bandits or any other dangers they faced. Surely he wasn't unnerved by this place.

Again, something nearby moaned.

Olga tried to smother her fear. She smiled. "Lots of magpies around. I keep hearing them."

"Those aren't magpies," Pavel said with a shake of his head. "People in my village used to tell stories of rusalki, spirits of those who drowned and would sing in order to lure people into

dangerous waters." Strangely, Pavel didn't seem the least per-
turbed by the idea of hearing spirits that might lure them to a
watery death in the nearby lake.

A rush of icy wind snatched at Olga's tunic. She spun
around, searching. Without waiting for her permission, her
heart's pace had quickened. An urge to call for help started
to creep into her throat, but she swallowed, trying to press it
down. It was a silly instinct—she had Pavel with her, and besides, she didn't need help from anyone. She would be fine.

The wind enveloped her, tight and suffocating. The leaves
on the trees rustled. She blinked, trying to clear the shadows
from her eyes.

There was movement between the trees. A ghostly figure,
pale as moonlight.

"See? I was right about the rusalki," whispered Pavel.

"They don't exist," Olga hissed. But still she hovered her
hands near her ears, ready to cover them at the first hint of a
bewitching song.

The creature shifted and Olga caught a glimpse of . . .

A swan.

She had to fight to hold back a laugh. An ordinary swan!
She stepped closer and saw a cluster of them, bowing their long
necks to drink from a trickle of water that must have escaped
a nearby stream.

"It seems we found the ghostly creatures in the valley," she
said with a smirk.

four

E ven though sundown was hours away, the shadows fell
quickly around Olga and Pavel. An unnatural murk obscured the path, clinging to the undergrowth. Soon the
gloom hung so heavy that it was almost impossible to keep
moving, even with the glow of Olga's heartstring.

"I think we should stop," said Pavel, setting down his pack.
"The stream has good water, and the ground is too uneven to
keep walking."

"We're so close to the palace. If we just go a bit farther . . . ,"
urged Olga.

"We don't know if we can even get into the palace. Come
on, Olga, we shouldn't be—"

But what they shouldn't be doing, Pavel didn't have a chance
to say. Eager to carry on, Olga had plunged deeper into the
trees, and she screamed as the ground crumbled away beneath
her feet.

She was sliding, plummeting down the steep cliff of a ravine.

Without time to think, Olga reached for her magic and yanked out a length of it, flinging it upward. The spell worked—it slowed her fall, and she managed to pull herself up. Her heart was pounding, her arms exhausted, but the magic lifted her, up and away, back toward where Pavel stood helpless on solid ground.

Panting, she crawled toward him. As she tried to stand, her leg gave out from under her. "My knee . . . ," she gasped as a shock of pain ran up the bone.

Pavel's face paled. He reached for Olga to steady her.

But it was too much. The magic, the shock, an injured leg. Dizziness overtook her, and she realized too late that she had used far too much magic in her panic.

Before she had a chance to wonder if Pavel would catch her, everything went dark.

Olga couldn't tell if she was dreaming or awake. She could feel herself being carried, hear soothing words spoken. She moaned and attempted to move, grasping some soft cloth. Voices murmured around her, going quiet when she cried out.

All around her was the familiar tingle of magic. But something was different—it hummed with a strange energy. It twisted and tangled. She reached out to unknot it, but she was too tired to lift her arms.

Savory smells wafted under her nose. Her stomach

grumbled, and she moaned again. How long had it been since she'd had a good meal?

Someone shushed her, a soft cooing that reminded her of a lullaby.

As she fell back asleep, she felt a tickle as an insect or a spider skittered over her hand. . . .

Olga woke in an unfamiliar room, on a bed so billowy with cloudlike blankets that she wondered for a moment if she was having some sort of heavenly vision. Maybe she was dead after all? She pinched her arm—that was what you were supposed to do, right? Her skin reddened and throbbed in response.

She looked around. If she wasn't dead, then she had somehow ended up in a dreamland. The bed frame filled a room that seemed to glimmer with flecks of gold on every surface. The wardrobe, the nightstand, the chairs and footstools. Each was constructed of deep red wood, densely carved with coils and vines. A full-length mirror occupied one corner of the room, tilted to reflect the firelight. The low fire murmured behind a grate decorated with gilt lilies, and warmth wrapped a comforting hold around her. A faint scent of roses hovered in the air.

Three windows spanned the room's full height on one wall. Just outside, a flock of golden birds swooped past. Through the glass, Olga spied an enormous garden at least three floors below. Beyond the garden wall was the tranquil lake.

Darkness had fallen and the bright moon had risen, lighting the hills and mountains that enclosed this place, with the lake resting between them.

She blinked, trying to remember what had happened. But the bed was the softest thing she had ever felt, and it took all her effort not to drift back asleep.

Her head ached. Everything ached. She tried to remember why.

Behind her eyelids there were sudden flashes of figures in the darkness. She was falling down the steep slope, her heart pounding. She'd been in the forest and used all her magic.

Now she was here. Where? She looked about the room again, at the embroidered upholstery of the chairs and mountainous pillows, the carved bed frame. There was only one place that she could be: the Sokolov Palace. She glanced out the window again, at the night sky. She must have been asleep for hours.

And where was Pavel? She had to find him.

She held a hand over her chest, checking how much her magic had replenished during her rest. She moved to get out of the bed. One of her knees was wrapped in stiff linen. She winced, remembering the pain in her leg. Who had bandaged her? Pavel wasn't good at that sort of thing. She maneuvered her leg and experienced no surge of pain. Nothing felt torn or out of place, so it seemed she'd narrowly missed doing any severe damage.

There was only one door, and no sooner had she sat up than it opened, and a tall figure sashayed over the threshold, a tea tray balanced in his arms.

His snow-white hair was combed back neatly, white

eyebrows like caterpillars on a soft, kind face. He spotted her and his rosy cheeks stretched into a smile.

"You're awake!" he said, surprised but not displeased. "I wanted to have these cookies ready and waiting for you!"

The tray was too large to fit on the bedside table, so he arranged it on a table near the fireplace and beckoned Olga closer.

"Are you hungry?" The tray held a teapot, cups, and a plate of golden cookies. A sweet, earthy scent swirled about the room, drawing Olga away from the bed. An expression of shock overtook the stranger as Olga approached. "I forgot to introduce myself! What terrible manners I have. I'm Baron Sokolov," he said, waving his hand with a practiced flourish. "I wish to welcome you to my home."

Olga gaped. She'd assumed he was a servant perhaps, or a doctor, not the owner of this extravagant place. And a baron at that. Was she supposed to curtsy? Surely there were rules about these things. But the baron didn't seem to mind that she hadn't.

"Th-thank you for the room," Olga stammered. She was unaccustomed to such a welcome. After so many years with Mr. Bulgakov, Olga was used to being either scolded or avoided. She looked down at the cookies and wondered whether she should feel delighted or suspicious.

Baron Sokolov continued, all exuberance and affability. "I thought you might like something sweet after the trial you've had." His blue eyes twinkled.

Olga paused for a moment to consider her answer. She and Pavel had hoped to find the palace empty, which it clearly was not.

Her first thought was to offer themselves as servants. It was a ruse that had worked several times with Mr. Bulgakov, because servants tended to go unnoticed by their masters. But she was being taken care of by the owner of the house himself, so there were no chances of pretending to be a servant and managing to search the house without him noticing.

Without waiting for her answer, the baron poured tea into two cups, splashing a little onto the tray. He withdrew a handkerchief and mopped up the excess. "Clumsy me!" he cried.

The scent of lavender and lemon filled the air as he offered her a teacup and the plate of cookies. Olga stared at the plate, uncertain at first, until her grumbling stomach finally convinced her that she was willing to overlook a lot of questions when cookies were involved.

She selected a cookie and took a small bite. Cinnamon and pepper and honey filled her nose and mouth. "These remind me of something. Maybe cookies my mother baked when I was very small." She fought the urge to gobble the entire thing in an instant and instead took another nibble, savoring it.

The baron gave a nod of understanding. "Smells can unlock all sorts of memories."

But Olga didn't want to talk about her mother, so she asked the baron, in as innocent a manner as possible: "How did I get here?"

"Your friend Pavel brought you," said the baron. He took his own teacup, his pinky sticking out as he pinched the handle.

"Is he okay?" she asked.

"Oh yes! He's downstairs enjoying the festivities." The baron returned the cup and saucer to the tray, then selected a cookie for himself, dusting the crumbs from his chest with his handkerchief as he nibbled.

Festivities? Olga frowned. Just how many people were here?

Her confusion must have shown on her face, because the baron smiled reassuringly. Pink cheeks flanked a mouth of dazzling white teeth. "He's at the ball. He didn't want to leave you, but I promised him that I would alert him as soon as you were awake." Then he noticed a smudge on a button of his doublet and stood to polish it with a little "Oh dear!"

The thought of Pavel enjoying himself while Olga lay injured in bed stung a little, and she felt a sharp pang of disappointment at being left out. She tried to swat the thought away. She needed to focus on the task at hand. If she wanted to find out about the Scarlet Heart, then Baron Sokolov was the only person who could tell her what she needed to know.

This was just like any of Mr. Bulgakov's schemes. He'd

always said that the first step in any plan was to understand the where and the who. She'd done this a hundred times before—never on her own, to be sure, but that didn't mean anything—and all she needed to do was treat the baron like another one of her past marks.

She watched him, taking in the sheen of his dancing shoes, the careful arrangement of the sash at his waist. The smudge he hadn't managed to buff from his button. "Thank you," she said, "for taking care of me."

The baron beamed at her. "You are most welcome. Please, stay as long as you need until you are fully recovered."

For the first time in a long time, Olga's winning smile was genuine. This was an invitation she was determined to use to her advantage.

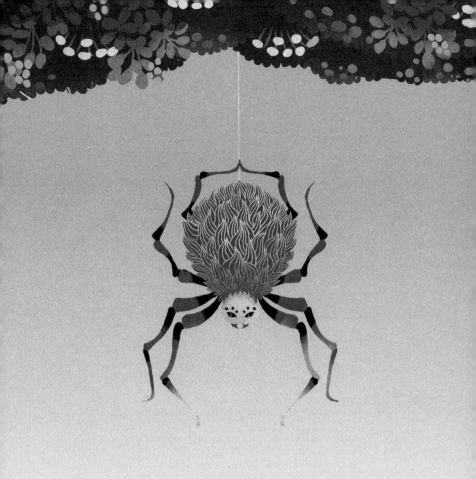

The Spider Spins
His Second Tale

I've told you, little ones, of the man who was first given the heartstring by the spider queen. I wish now to tell you of another man from this valley. You must steel your nerves, little ones, and prepare for something dreadful.

This second man was descended from the first. He was born in a great palace. And like his ancestor, this man had the ability to see and wield heartstrings. But he also saw a new potential in them: His heartstring gave him an advantage over others. And this made him hungry for power.

It wasn't long before he began to suspect that it was possible for him to become even as powerful as the tsar. And so the young man began to train himself in magic, warping and bending it, pulling magic further than it had ever been stretched before. After many years he realized that he could use other people's heartstrings for his own spells—a frightful discovery!

He married a woman who also practiced magic, a woman whose beauty was known throughout the tsardom. Their life was one of pleasure and power. They invited people to their palace, hosting balls every night, and every guest who saw them marveled at the depth of their love. Together they flaunted their magic, demonstrating how easily they could manipulate their surroundings. She studied as relentlessly as he did. It seemed the man had found a partner whose skill rivaled his own.

Until something changed between them. It happened when the man's wife learned she was having a baby. What a source for joy this should have been!

He saw this as a chance to fulfill his life's aim. Their child would also have magic—there could be no doubt of that. And as the child of two heartstringers, it was bound to have power beyond even the man's own. This would be his path to claiming the tsardom.

But the news of their growing family held a different meaning for his wife. She became less interested in magic, devoting herself instead to building a comfortable home for their child. She went weeks without visiting their laboratory.

The baby grew in the wife's belly, and the man looked forward to the power this child would bring him. His wife begged him to reconsider this plan. It would place their child in danger. Their baby needed a father who was loving and devoted. He needed to let go of his hunger.

But he ignored her pleas. His plans became his sole focus, and he spent many hours writing and studying. He often didn't return to his bedroom before dawn.

Until one day, his wife was gone. She had disappeared in the night.

But she had left a spell of her own, one that tied him to the valley so that he could never leave in search of her.

So I ask you, little ones: what becomes of a heartstring that is used for power instead of love?

five

B aron Sokolov watched the window, and the light glinted in his white hair. "The ball ends at sunrise. Might you join me as I bid my guests good night?" He withdrew a pocket watch and examined it.

Olga couldn't think of anything she wanted to do less than leave this cozy room for a crowded ballroom. But following the baron was the perfect way to better explore the palace, and she needed to talk to Pavel.

Trying to feign enthusiasm, she nodded.

"Wonderful!" said the baron. "There are some clothes in the wardrobe that you can change into. They might be a little large, but not overly so. They once belonged to my wife." Something passed across his face as he said this, a darkness that Olga couldn't recognize or unravel. And then it was gone.

Olga was used to reading people, unearthing the hidden clues in their expressions. And there were a thousand buried thoughts in the baron's words.

"I think I'd like to stay in my own clothes, if you please," Olga said, trying to match his easy manner of speech.

The baron gave her a quizzical look but quickly shook off his surprise at Olga's indifference to ball gowns. With a bow, he extended his arm to her, and Olga took it. They left through another door and sauntered down a long corridor. Olga was relieved to find she could walk without pain from her injury.

With each step they took, the palace seemed determined to impress. Candlelight from the chandeliers twinkling overhead beckoned Olga forward. Draped on the walls were enormous tapestries depicting scenes of celebration. From the end of the corridor, music trilled and laughter echoed.

The corridor opened to a hall large enough to contain an entire house. A grand staircase led down to glossy marble floors. Five sets of doors stood open, the left two leading into what appeared to be a banquet hall, the doors on the right opening to the ballroom. Voices echoed around the chamber. Olga flinched a little—she'd always found the cacophony of crowded rooms to be like scratches on her skin—but then the music began to play, and it filled her with something warm and familiar.

Baron Sokolov led her down the stairs and through the lefthand doors. The air was thick with the aroma of blackened grouse with wild mushrooms, cheesecakes, and tangy cream with sea buckthorn berries—foods that Olga had always imagined tasting but had only ever seen and smelled from a distance. Some people were seated at tables, but many stood as they ate, taking food from servants with trays of canapés. When a servant came with pancakes stacked with caviar alongside

crayfish garnished with dill and fennel, the baron held the tray
for her so that she wouldn't have to decide what she wanted and
could instead have some of everything.

They ate as they ventured into the ballroom, and it wasn't
long before she spotted Pavel dancing in the center of the as-
sembly with a pretty young lady. When the dance ended,
another lass was eager to take the place of the first, and Olga
realized there was a cluster of girls waiting to dance with him.
A broad smile lit his face, and his partners looked every bit
as delighted by him as he was with them. He was a natural
dancer, moving with the elegance that his training in fighting
provided him, and it was clear that the line of ladies was much
longer than the remaining time before sunrise.

A familiar sensation tugged at her. The same feeling she'd

had when she'd first set eyes on the lake, of something pulling at her, threatening to sweep her away. She tried to hold on to her thoughts but could feel them drifting from her, drawn by the music and the movement and the flicker of candlelight.

There was something she'd meant to talk to Pavel about, but now that he was before her, she struggled to remember. Something to do with why they were here . . .

She fought to clear her mind but felt herself being dazzled by the beauty of the ballroom and the twirling of people on the dance floor. The baron seemed determined to tell Olga the name of every dish on the banquet table, to describe the origin of every flower in each elaborate arrangement, and to introduce Olga to every person in the room. He brought guests to meet her, one after the other. He introduced the people nearby with names Olga didn't really care to remember. There was a man with golden skin and a trim black beard. His angular limbs pointed sideways as he sipped kvass. A round woman with a peachy smiling face and hair the color of molasses. Twin boys who didn't seem to be much older than Olga herself. A young woman around Pavel's age, with long dark hair and eyes as round as the cookie Olga was holding.

For this last introduction, the baron said, "My dears! What a delight! Olga, this is Anna. She arrived only a few days before you and Pavel. I am certain you will get along famously."

It didn't seem possible, but Anna's eyes grew even rounder, and her face broke into a beaming grin as she reached for Olga's hand. Before Olga could find somewhere to put the cookie, she found it being crushed into crumbs under Anna's enthusiastic handshake.

"Oh, how wonderful!" Anna said. "I know we shall be dear friends. It is just like a book I read once, where a princess and a village girl meet in a ballroom and become as close as a flock of starlings. You're the princess, of course, not I. You have beautiful curls just like a princess." She paused with a small gasp of breath and suddenly remembered, "However, in the story they battle a dragon, but we can find our own activities—what do you think?"

The flow of words hit Olga like a blast of wind. One thing was certain: there was no reason for her and Anna to become friends. She nodded indifferently and said nothing.

The baron seemed to pick up on Olga's discomfort, because he said, "Let us return you to Pavel, my dear!" before leading Anna away.

"Oh yes! Pavel is so kind and welcoming! It's wonderful that you host a ball every night—I've never had the chance to meet so many people at once before. . . ."

Olga watched them depart with a sense of relief. While the others in the room enjoyed talking and laughing and dancing, she found pleasure in the luxury surrounding her. The emerald curtains threaded with gold, the moldings clinging to the windows and ceiling. Faces peered from paintings in gilded frames, and the perfume of exotic jasmine danced past her nose.

Idly, she studied how the baron wove through the room. Olga watched his rosy cheeks, the swish of his cloak, the glint in his eyes as he greeted each of his guests and offered refreshments with an openness that put everyone at ease.

She observed the guests he'd introduced. The way the

candlelight twinkled on the skin and beard of the angular man. How the sapphire-studded hems of the round woman's gown accentuated her eyes and the deeper tones of her hair. It was hard to tell, but there was something about these people that felt unusual, unexpected, like they'd been woven of two different types of thread. But the closer she looked, the more the answer eluded her.

Pavel appeared before her, dashing in a purple velvet waistcoat. The baron must have given him clothes, just like he'd offered to let Olga borrow his wife's gowns.

"Olga!" Pavel half shouted. "Come dance!" He held the hand of Anna, who radiated so much delight that Olga couldn't stare directly at them.

"Oh yes!" cried Anna. "Do join! Can you imagine if we all had to dance because the floor was covered in hot coals or because we were forced to wear iron shoes? I read that in a story once. What a strange dance that would be!"

The music for the next dance had begun, and Pavel moved into the circuit as though the tide had carried him from Olga, jolting her out of the floating feeling she'd been enjoying. She suddenly remembered that they'd come to this place with a purpose.

When Pavel returned after the dance, she pulled him aside to see if he'd discovered any useful clues from his dance partners. "Have any of them mentioned seeing the jewel?"

He laughed in a way that usually reassured Olga and filled her with warmth when she was worried. "Mr. Bulgakov isn't here," he said. "It's okay to do something that isn't *according to plan.*" Then he was borne away again before Olga could reply.

Someone offered Olga a tray of food, and without even realizing, Olga took a bite. Before long, she was wholly focused on the earthy tastes of toasted chestnuts and potatoes with dollops of rich soured cream, sprouts with hazelnuts, beets with sweet and zesty pomegranate seeds.

The past couple of days had been taxing. First being chased out of the village, then leaving Mr. Bulgakov. Not to mention nearly plummeting to her death over a cliff. What could it hurt to enjoy herself for one night? She could eat her fill, then rest and begin searching in the morning. . . .

When the baron stepped into the center of the room, she watched him, as eager as all the other guests to hear the speech that would conclude the festivities for the night.

"Friends!" the baron announced, and his voice rang through the room. "We welcome two new guests to our nightly revelry! I hope you will make them feel at home." His blue eyes landed on Olga as he said the final words, "For however long they are with us."

six

Olga woke, stiff and groggy, in the same room as the night before, with no memory of returning to it after the baron's speech had concluded the ball. Sunlight peeped through the curtains to land on the puff of bedclothes and pillows surrounding her. She laid her head back and closed her eyes, trying to picture the bright colors, the swishing dresses, the chorus of pipes and violins. Like fog burning away in the sunlight, her memories were rapidly evaporating from her mind.

She fought to hold on to them. Last night, she had discovered that a valley that was supposed to be deserted and a palace thought to be abandoned were not only occupied but brimming with life. The baron hosted balls here *every night*.

Who were the guests? How had they managed to keep this secret from the outside world? And why was she being so warmly welcomed when no one knew a thing about her?

Everything about the ball, about this *place*, seemed strange.

Worst of all, it would be too easy for the balls to distract her from her mission. The baron, with his twinkling eyes and rosy cheeks, hosting nightly balls for a swarm of feather-brained aristocrats . . . he was her target. He seemed to delight in the attention of his guests—was there a chance he'd neglected to keep careful watch over his treasures? Or perhaps that warm geniality disguised a hidden cleverness, something Olga would have to be wary of. And why would he give a ball every night? In all her travels, she'd never heard of anyone hosting so many gatherings.

Olga needed to discuss a new plan with Pavel. Planning always gave her a feeling of composure, as if stepping out of squishy mud and onto dry hard stone. She felt in control when she had a list of things to do next.

The western sunlight streaming into the room indicated that it was now well into the afternoon, and she admonished herself for sleeping so late. Half a day of searching the palace for the Scarlet Heart already gone. So she rose from the bed and quickly washed herself in the tub placed in the corner of her room. The water was perfectly warm, infused with the rose petals floating on its surface. A set of combs had been laid out on a table next to the mirror, and she tugged them through the tangles in her hair. She felt lighter somehow, all thoughts now directed toward finding Pavel and finding the jewel.

Out of curiosity she peeked into the wardrobe to see the dresses the baron had told her about. She felt a twinge of jealousy at the fine stitching of a blue gown embroidered with a pattern of copper leaves, and the needlework on a dainty reticule of daisy yellow with purple petals and vines. For years she had attempted to stitch and sew, but it was something she did on Mr. Bulgakov's orders. Her sewing was poor, and only through illusion did it resemble anything people considered worth purchasing.

If she found the jewel, she would never have to sew—or swindle—again.

The dresses were far more extravagant than Olga felt comfortable wearing. She'd spent too many years sneaking into places where she didn't belong, avoiding attention, to change her ways now. So she closed the wardrobe doors and returned to her old clothes and satchel, patched and worn as they were.

On the previous night, the baron had directed her right, toward the ballroom. Now Olga turned left, hoping the halls would lead her away from other guests while she explored.

As Olga rounded a corner, she almost collided with Pavel. He clasped a tankard of some liquid in his large hands.

"Oh, good!" Olga said with relief at finding him so soon. "Is your room nearby?"

Pavel nodded, his fiery hair falling into his eyes. "Just back that way. I'm coming from *one of* the breakfast rooms." His eyes widened at such extravagance.

Olga's stomach grumbled. The treats from the ball now felt like a long time ago.

"Here," said Pavel, handing her the tankard. "It's a pear cider, your favorite."

Olga sniffed it, enjoying the bubbles that tickled her nose. "If it's half as good as the food at the ball, I could drink three more of these."

"How are your blini?" he asked as she took a sip.

The cider was perfect—bursting with pear and cinnamon

and honey. As soon as she swallowed, she took another gulp, savoring the floating feeling it delivered. Finally, she remembered that Pavel had asked a question, and she answered. "Never better."

Olga's stomach gurgled again. Pavel was too polite to tease her. Instead, he wrapped an arm around her shoulder and began to lead her down the corridor and through a set of double doors. They crossed the threshold into air that was thick with smells of smoky black tea, sausages, and cheese dumplings.

A bright room greeted them, empty except for a table laden with treats. Some of the foods were familiar, but there were also exotic-looking pastries and vibrant fruits Olga didn't recognize. Olga picked up a tube-shaped pastry and took an eager bite, its heat steaming on her tongue and the crust leaving flecks on her lips. Pumpkin and cheese, with dandelion greens and a hint of nutmeg. She recognized all the flavors but had never had them together before, and her heart stuttered as she realized she might never be satisfied by hard traveling bread and stolen eggs after flavors such as these.

But as she ate, it suddenly struck her just how *quiet* everything was, silent enough to feel like she could sense the heartbeat of this place. No servants standing in corners, no courtiers flitting between rooms in day dresses and riding clothes. It was possible they were all still asleep after the festivities of the night before, but it did seem strange not to see *someone* else enjoying breakfast. The table was filled with food, yet there was no one but Olga and Pavel to eat it.

Her gaze swept the room, taking in the candelabras with crystals that twinkled in the morning light and painted rainbows on the walls. Gold threads glimmered from drapes adorning the windows, and enormous arrangements of roses and lilies dotted the room. A clock on the mantelpiece chimed with a familiar tune. She'd never been somewhere so impressive, so . . . perfect.

Too perfect.

How could it be that a palace rumored to be abandoned was instead a dreamland of feasts and festivities? After so many years with Mr. Bulgakov, Olga had learned that perfection couldn't be trusted. She had crafted enough illusions to know. Something was always hidden underneath.

"Olga?" said Pavel, a nervous lilt to his voice. "Are you okay? You look . . . odd."

She jolted at his question, feeling an almost imperceptible snap. And then nothing. Whatever she'd been worried about escaped her.

She was probably just imagining things.

"We need to start searching for the jewel," she said in answer. "It'll be risky with so many guests—we'll want to be careful not to get caught." She looked around them at the empty room, wondering what risk there actually was of being seen. But it was best to be cautious. "And I think we shouldn't go to tonight's ball. It'd give us more time to explore while everyone is in the ballroom."

But Pavel shuffled his feet. "I was hoping . . ." He paused and took a breath, beginning again. "Could we search before the ball? It's just . . . I had fun."

Olga winced. She wasn't sure she wanted to attend the ball again. She had enjoyed herself. Maybe too much. The food, the music—she wanted more of it. Wanted more of the sensation she kept discovering in this place, as if she were staring at a bright sun and desperately trying to view it in its full wonder and glory. She didn't like the way she couldn't quite tell when she woke whether she was still dreaming. Sometimes she thought she caught snippets of familiar songs in the air.

But her fears were silly. They weren't based on anything real—it was just a hunch, nervousness maybe.

"Fine," she agreed, eager to begin searching. The faster they searched, the sooner they could leave this place. "If we don't find anything, we ask around for clues at the ball. Discreetly!"

They both knew that the jewel wasn't likely to be kept anywhere obvious like a bedroom. Somewhere there would be a hidden vault—behind a tapestry, under a floorboard. So instead of searching the upstairs rooms, Olga suggested they make their way downward.

Just outside the door to the breakfast room stood a curling set of stairs. As Olga reached for the banister, something moved, some little creature skittering away from her palm. Pavel yelped as it ducked into a shadowy corner. He hated anything with more than four legs.

"Ready?" Olga asked.

He gave another shudder but nodded. "If I had a palace like this, I'd make sure it had no pests anywhere," he grumbled.

Olga bit back her laugh, and together they followed the steps down. The stairs landed at another hall lined with candles and open doors.

"No chances of barging in on sleeping guests here," Olga said. "Ready to search?"

Pavel gave a hopeful shrug. "One by one. Room by room."

The first room appeared to be a gallery. Portraits of severe-looking ancestors of Baron Sokolov stood guard over the furniture. A man with a bushy mustache sat with a white hound by his knee. A group of ladies wearing towering powdered wigs were frozen in the middle of a dance. Olga and Pavel studied each portrait, touching the frames to see if their fingers bumped any knobs or switches. At the end of the row, the wall was bare, a faint outline visible where a painting had once been. Olga pressed the wallpaper, feeling for any cracks, but there was nothing.

They continued on to the next room, where musical instruments lined the walls. They opened the lid of the harpsichord and peered inside flutes. Pavel lifted a lute from the wall under the pretense of checking that nothing was hidden behind it, but he couldn't help himself. He strummed the strings.

"Put that back! What if someone hears you?" Olga snapped.

His ears flushed pink and he returned it to its hook on the shelf.

Together they followed passages and stairways, quickly discovering the palace apparently had a room for everything. They found an armory, a room filled floor to ceiling with sewing supplies and fabrics, plus multiple sitting rooms, dining rooms, lavatories, and larders.

Strange sounds followed them on their search. More than once they turned a corner and Olga was sure she heard the rustle of sudden movement, as though someone had been waiting for them and run when they appeared.

During their search of the ground floor, it became clear

that there were lower levels of the palace, stairs leading down to cellars—"Or maybe a secret passage!" said Pavel hopefully.

The corridors here were shrouded in shadows, absent of windows.

Something scurried behind them and Olga froze, watching movement slice through the gloom of the corridor. It slipped around a corner and was gone. She waited a moment for whatever it was to return, but when it did not, she motioned to a confused Pavel that they should continue down the hall, refusing to let herself think about who or what she'd just seen.

They navigated down, down, as far as they could go, where a labyrinthine series of passages would make it easy to get lost if they weren't careful.

They came to a landing where cold pressed against Olga's skin and the air was thick with dust. Before them was an ancient-looking door made of heavy ironwood, its hinges rusted. There were traces of rat droppings near the base.

Pavel managed to pull the door open, the wood and hinges groaning, to reveal yet another staircase curving down. The stone steps were dry and cracked. The shadows were solid and dark as a grave.

His light green eyes absorbed the gloom. "Are you sure you want to go down here?" he asked.

"You have your knife, right? And I have my lock picks and torch," she said, motioning toward the flicker of magic she could feel in her chest, and withdrawing a strand to light their way.

"Yes," Pavel agreed.

"And we've been in much tighter spots than a dank cellar, right?" she said.

Pavel couldn't deny that.

"I could go by myself, if you prefer?" she said playfully.

That did it. Pavel wasn't about to let Olga descend into the creepy passage alone.

Together they stepped into the darkness.

seven

lowly they descended step by step. Olga couldn't shake the feeling that there must be something worth hiding in these hidden depths. Rough walls scraped against Olga's knuckles and the pads of her fingers as she let them guide her ever downward. Her nose prickled from the dusty air. Only the sounds of their shallow breaths and cautious footsteps disturbed the silence.

As they reached the bottom of the stairs, a corridor stretched out before them, just visible in the pale glow of Olga's heartstring. On one side the wall was covered with stone plaques carved with names.

BARON NIKOLAI SOKOLOV

1654–1716

BARON PYOTR SOKOLOV

1487–1559

On and on they went, each emblazoned with a small insignia of a spider.

This was no treasury; this was a crypt. Behind her, Pavel shivered.

But Olga had to wonder if perhaps these people had been buried with their treasures alongside them. Olga moved toward one of the plaques, running her fingers over the engraving.

How far was she prepared to go to find what she wanted?

"Olga . . . ," whispered Pavel.

She placed her palm flat against the cold stone, as if she could feel the heartbeat of the person in their grave.

As she did, she heard a skittering. She turned, searching for a sign of movement. There, along the wall, she caught a glimpse of something running. It moved in the shadows again, and she whirled around, scrambling to find the comforting tingle of magic in her chest before she hurled it at the flicking movement.

Her magic scorched the air before finding its target. Her hand closed around something wiggling and fuzzy, and she nearly dropped it but instead squeezed tighter.

"OW!" the thing shouted.

This time Olga did drop whatever it was, and she blinked as it scuttled away from her across the dusty floor.

"No you don't," Olga muttered, and she reached out, the magic still attached to the creature and forming a leash between them. She held firm, pulling whatever it was back toward her as though she were reeling in a fish on a hook.

"Ow, stop! How are you doing that?!" said the voice. "Let me go!"

"Not until I find out what you are," said Olga. With a final tug, she pulled the thing back into her hand and closed her fingers around it. She clasped it close to her face and opened her fist so that she could see the thing on her flattened palm.

It was an enormous spider. Black, hairy, with glittering eyes.

Next to her Pavel squirmed, holding in a whine. She closed her hand most of the way so Pavel couldn't see, knowing how much he hated spiders.

Olga narrowed her own eyes at the creature. Spiders didn't frighten her. But never, in her whole life, had she heard a spider *talk*.

"What do you want?" the spider shrieked. Its many legs jittered. Olga wasn't sure if spiders had knees, but if they did, this one's were quaking.

"How are you talking to me?" Olga demanded, then turned to Pavel. "Did you hear it too?"

Pavel looked like he was about to throw up, his face green in the pale light.

"I'm a *he,* not an *it.* And you have no right to capture me," said the spider. "Now let me go!"

The spider crouched as though he was about to leap from Olga's palm, but Olga grabbed him.

"How?!" Olga demanded.

"Would you stop grabbing me?" said the spider. "It makes me nervous, and I can't think when I'm nervous."

"If I set you down," said Olga, "you'll answer my questions?"

The spider gave a strange bob of his hairy body that was unmistakably a nod.

Slowly, Olga bent down and lowered the spider to the floor.

In a flash, the spider took off, disappearing through a crack between the wall and the floor. There might have been an excited giggle that sounded as he escaped, though Olga wasn't quite sure, as she'd never heard a spider giggle before. But she couldn't blame him for celebrating his escape, or for laughing at Olga for falling for such an obvious trick.

They might not have found treasure, but it confirmed what she'd already suspected: there were far more secrets in this place than she'd anticipated.

Pavel was eager to return aboveground after that. Olga panted as she followed his brisk steps, taking the stairs two at a time. "I just need to walk," Pavel said.

Olga understood. Pavel was the kind of person who felt better after running around and jumping a bit.

At last they emerged into the entrance hall, where windows three stories high presented the garden topiaries just outside. The doors to the ballroom and banquet hall were currently closed, as were the enormous front doors of the palace.

With quick steps, Pavel and Olga approached the entrance. A large metal latch took most of Olga's strength to lower, and then Pavel pulled at the ring, grunting as the heavy doors swung open. Together they stepped out into the garden. The afternoon sun threw shadows over the paths lined with hedges that towered over them, and the light scent of violets danced in the air. There was a relief at being outside again, feeling the warmth of sunshine brushing her cheeks and the breeze whispering in her ears.

Olga looked back up at the outside of the palace, wondering if it was possible that there was nothing particularly special for her to find. The building stretched along the lakeshore, longer than the main street of a small village and tall enough to contain at least six stories. Dotted along the roof were towers and turrets, their peaks blending with the distant mountains behind them. Hundreds of windows gave glimpses of the thousands of candles inside, the window frames decorated with gold leaf and blossoming vines. There were treasures to be found here, that was certain. But were any of them jewels fit for the tsar?

As if in answer to her question, there was a piercing screech. It had come from the direction of the forest, beyond the garden walls. The screech hadn't sounded human, but it was hard to be sure.

She turned to Pavel and was grateful to see the worry in his eyes as well.

The cry sounded again. Before she had time to react, Pavel was striding down the path. With some reluctance, she followed him to the far side of the garden, where a gate opened out to the forest on their left and the lakeshore on their right.

The cry seemed to be coming from the trees. Pavel stepped toward it. Something moved, jostling branches.

It was one of the swans, flapping with jittery, erratic movements. The bird was stuck in a tangle of brambles.

Pavel gasped and rushed forward into the thicket. The swan batted its wings fearfully at him. Blood dripped down its legs from the thorns.

"It's okay. I want to help," Pavel said. He hummed a soft tune, one that Olga had often heard him play. He began to sing the words in his low, soothing voice.

"How the stars stir at the sounds of her cries. . . ."

But as he reached to help the swan, something caught Olga's eye. She blinked, wondering if she had imagined it. But there it was again, something shimmering, wound tight about the bird's neck and belly, constricting its wings.

"Pavel, wait!" Olga said. "There's magic here."

She could see them clearly now, strands crisscrossing around the swan, wrapping it tightly. There were so many, it was almost like the swan was trapped in a cocoon or wearing a cloak. It was more magic than she'd ever seen in one place.

"We can't just leave it like this," said Pavel. "What if the magic is hurting it?"

"You don't know what that magic is for!" As she said this, something moaned on the breeze. *OooEEEaaaooo.* The sound was carried from the forest, and at first Olga thought it was nothing more than the wind in the trees. But there it was again. Soft. Musical. Mournful.

Olga remembered hearing the same cry as she and Pavel had traveled through the woods to the palace. She had thought the sound came from swans. Now Olga looked at the swan before her. It screeched and trumpeted its pain. Nearby, more swans floated on the surface of the lake, emitting only low trills and honks.

The moans in the forest weren't coming from the swans. There was something else out there.

Pavel ignored her warning, gently prying away branches, careful to keep any thorns away from the creature's flesh. "There you are," he told it. "You're safe now."

The swan limped back toward the lake, leaving a trail of blood from the wounds on its legs and wings. It attempted to fly but struggled to stay in the air for long and landed near the edge of the water. Several other swans were clustered close by, all floating together near the lakeshore. Olga could no longer see the strands of magic, and for a moment she began to wonder if she had imagined them.

She eyed the swans warily. There was nothing to be frightened of. They were simply swans.

But Olga was remembering the feeling she'd had in the

breakfast room, the tug she'd felt at the edge of the valley, the talking spider. Her instincts were telling her not to return to the ballroom, not to trust the sights and sounds of this place. And for the first time she wondered if she had been too quick to dismiss Mr. Bulgakov's warnings.

The Spider Spins
His Third Tale

You must have realized by now, little ones, that the stories I tell you weave a history of this valley. And you may have guessed that these tales lead inevitably to the curse that almost destroyed our home. Let me answer your curiosity, little ones, with the story of a swan.

This swan desired nothing more than a peaceful life. Free from hunters, with plentiful food. She sought a never-ending haze of drifting across the still surface of her lake and sleeping in nearby gardens.

And for as long as the swan could remember, this dream had been her reality. The swan was never hungry, or tired, or frightened.

Yet the swan was surprised to notice that sometimes members of her flock left the lake, and she could not understand why. Why would anyone leave such bliss? But leave they did. It happened seldom, but enough to make the swan worry. Had her missing kin found someplace better? Or had they come to harm?

One day the swan saw something white in the woods near the lakeshore. She swam closer, curious, and saw many figures clustered. The figures moved, and the swan followed. The swan left the water and waddled toward the woods. She spread her wings to fly low between the trees.

A blinding pain. The swan screeched. Not a hunter's arrow,

just a thicket of brambles, but the swan was stuck. She tried to move, and the thorns tore at her flesh. She cried again.

Two humans answered, and though the swan first suspected a trap, her fears were unfounded. The humans freed the swan. She hobbled on a bloody foot and floated on scratched wings back toward the water.

The swan was angry at herself for her own curiosity. If she hadn't gone near the woods, this wouldn't have happened! Once again she wished for a life that was nothing more than a dreamy stream of happiness, floating on the lake, watching the sun rise and set. Days blending together to form a cloud of unending tranquility.

But the pain in her leg had punctured that dream. And the faces of those humans had stirred something in the swan's heart, memories that were unfamiliar and forbidden.

The swan didn't want to dwell on any such pain. She wanted to forget.

Now I ask you, little ones, is such a peace worth pursuing?

eight

"There's some sort of magic here," said Olga. "The balls.
The spider. The swans. It could be dangerous."

She and Pavel had returned to her room. Olga paced
before the fire, feeling the heat from the flames against her
ankles, taking comfort in the certainty that the fire was *real*.

"Magic doesn't mean this place is dangerous. You have
magic too," said Pavel, more calm than Olga, his hands resting on his knees. Magic didn't make him uneasy the way it
did some strangers, and Pavel had always accepted Olga's rare
ability as a simple fact of life.

"At best it's a distraction from finding the jewel," said Olga,
"or else an intentional way of concealing it. We need to be careful. And focused."

"*Or* it could be exactly what we needed," said Pavel simply.
"We were looking for treasure because it would offer us a different kind of life. But now we're here, and we can dance and
eat and sing and do anything we wish. Isn't that the new life
we wanted?"

"I don't trust it," she mumbled.

There was a long pause. Finally, Pavel said, "Yes, but you don't trust anything."

Her cheeks burned. It was true—she didn't trust people. But that was because she couldn't. People looked out for themselves, no matter who else got hurt.

So forgetting about the jewel and enjoying the balls was out of the question for her. They needed to follow their plan and leave as soon as they could.

The lacy magic of this place was protecting something. And she had to follow the strands to figure out what.

Pavel went off to get ready for the ball, while Olga spent the next hour searching her room for signs of magic, hoping to find a thread that would lead them to the jewel like a trail of bread crumbs.

A skittering sound interrupted her thoughts. She turned, searching for a sign of movement. There, along the wall! She caught a glimpse of something running.

She was sure it was the spider.

"Wait, come back here!" she said, now knowing that the spider could understand her and speak back if he wished.

Olga spotted the spider running along the rug. "I said *stop!*" she shouted. But the spider only ran faster.

The rope of magic she'd tried to lasso around the creature

fizzed as it missed its mark. Not wanting to lose sight of him again, Olga threw herself at the spider, arms outstretched, cupping her hands over his small, skittering body. "Gotcha," she said triumphantly.

The spider squirmed. "Let me go," squeaked the voice. "Unhand me. I demand it."

"What are you doing here? Why have you been following me?" Olga said. "I won't let you go until I have answers."

"I've done nothing," said the spider.

"Are you spying for someone? Guarding secrets? What do you know?"

"I know many things," said the spider, "and I've seen things that are better left undisturbed."

That all sounded a bit dramatic. "What's that supposed to mean?" Olga asked.

The spider straightened his legs, drawing his small body to its fullest height. "Your curiosity is going to get you into trouble."

"Is that a threat?"

"No! It's a warning."

"I can look after myself," said Olga, annoyance creeping into her voice. "What kind of trouble?"

The spider trembled a little, taking his time before replying. "There are things happening in this valley—rumblings, murmurs. I came from the forest to investigate."

"Is that why you're following me around? You think I caused it?" Olga asked.

"No, I don't."

"Then why would I interest you so much?"

The spider was silent, considering. "Because the visitors who come here never leave."

Mr. Bulgakov's warning echoed in Olga's mind. "Why? How?"

"It's what I'm trying to find out. A web of shadow stretches over this valley, magic unlike anything I've ever seen. It's distorted, infected."

"Do you think it's connected to the swans? Or the ball-room?" Had the spider noticed the same signs Olga had? Could they pool their information?

"It's everywhere. That's why it's been impossible to find the source. There are so many threads, all matted and tangled— I can't find where they lead."

"So you're searching the palace?" asked Olga. When the spider bobbed his body in a nod, she continued, "Well, so am I. We should help each other."

"Help? With what?" The spider suddenly sounded indignant.

"I'll help you follow the strings if you'll help me find the jewel, the Scarlet Heart." The spider would be able to check nooks and crannies that Olga and Pavel couldn't reach. And Olga had a feeling—an instinct—that the threads were connected to the jewel somehow. She'd felt the magic when she'd first looked at the valley with Mr. Bulgakov. It was like the threads were meant to lead her somewhere, to help her find what she was looking for.

"I'm not sure if I should," said the spider.

"Why not? What are you afraid of?"

"My queen wouldn't want me distracted."

Queen? Olga nearly asked, then decided she didn't really want to know. If she and the spider could help each other search, that was all that mattered.

"I've sensed the magic, and I can help you," Olga went on. "You'll move faster if you ride with me." She held out a pocket of her shirt.

The spider thought for a long moment. "You will help me find the source of the spells?"

"We'll search the palace together," Olga said in answer. No need to make promises she couldn't keep.

The spider seemed to be warming to the idea as he crawled up Olga's arm and sat on her shoulder. The tickle of his legs made her skin tingle. "It is an excellent view from here," he said. Then he crawled down Olga's chest to enter a pocket.

"What should I call you?" Olga asked.

"Pauk suits me well enough," said the spider.

"I'm Olga. So we have a deal?" Olga asked.

They couldn't shake on it, but a verbal agreement would have to do.

Olga smiled to herself. She wasn't about to tell Pavel that she'd just made an alliance with a spider.

From somewhere deep within the palace, a bell tolled. The ball would begin shortly. Pavel would be there, but Olga wanted to use this chance to continue her explorations.

"Where did you last search?" said Olga.

Inside Olga's pocket, the spider shivered.

"What's wrong?" asked Olga.

"I don't want to go back there," Pauk said.

Olga bit back a groan. "Why?"

"It was a dangerous place for spiders."

What does that mean? Olga thought, but instead, she said, "Er, okay, what if you just tell me where to go?"

The spider trembled but finally relented. Pointing the way with a spindly leg, he directed Olga out of her room. Together they navigated unfamiliar corridors over carpets that were snowy with dust. The spider pointed and Olga followed, down winding staircases and through unlit rooms with doors concealed behind tapestries, into a wing of the palace Olga hadn't explored yet.

They entered a conservatory, an orangery, and then a greenhouse. The heavy scent of orchids filled Olga's nose, and she stumbled on a trailing vine. She pushed against a door and entered a dark hallway. In the air was a faint rhythm of chirps and trills, which crescendoed as she approached another door at the end of the corridor.

Olga blinked, wondering where Pauk had led her, when suddenly she spotted it: a seemingly forgotten filament, frayed and translucent, trailing along the floor.

Nearly clapping in delight, Olga reached out to touch the strand. She could feel it just as distinctly as her own heartstring, though this strand was thin and brittle. She hesitated to hold it lest it fall apart in her hands. The strand wound under the closed door at the end of the hall.

Fingers trembling with excitement, Olga pushed the door open. The passage opened to a room that seemed as though it couldn't decide whether it was indoors or out. A dense copse of trees stood, their branches thick with late-summer leaves. In lieu of a ceiling, intricate wires formed a lattice cage that

curved up into a dome overhead. For a moment, Olga thought the entire structure was made of glass, but then she noticed how the tree branches pierced the cage, and birds zoomed through the frame into the lavender sunset. Everywhere there were birds, peeping from branches, clinging to the metal frame, swinging and swooping. Large parrots, tiny hummingbirds. Finches flitted and cranes stretched their long legs. Yet more birds were on the ground—swans waddled between benches, peacocks strutted around stones. Sitting in one of the chairs, sipping a dark wine, was Baron Sokolov.

Olga felt the spider scurry into her pocket.

The baron stood, his posture relaxed, his arms open in welcome. "Come in! I see you have found my aviary."

The tension in Olga's shoulders didn't ease at his welcome.

She had hoped to find the room empty so she could search it properly. But finding him here offered its own information. She watched him as he stood to give her a cordial bow, hoping his movements would signal something useful. People had a tendency to look at things that were important to them when they thought others weren't paying attention.

"It's beautiful," said Olga, working to imitate his easy manner. "How many birds do you have?"

From her pocket, Olga heard Pauk whisper, "Can we get out of here? Birds like to *eat* spiders!" But Olga hissed between her teeth, hoping the spider would take the hint to be quiet. Being here felt like the right track toward finding the jewel.

The baron clearly hadn't noticed their interaction, answering Olga's question without pause. "More than fifty species!" he said spiritedly. "Many rare and exotic. My favorites are the swans you see here." He gestured to the group of swans clustered around a small water fixture. "They may seem common, but they are a species entirely unique to this palace."

The mention of the swans caught Olga's attention. Looking closer and squinting, she could just glimpse strands of magic flickering among them. Aside from the swans, none of the other birds showed any trace of magic.

OooEEEaaaooo.

The familiar cry came from the forest outside the aviary. She took a step forward, half tempted to peer through the aviary's gate leading out to the surrounding grounds.

But the baron was looking at the watch he'd pulled from his pocket. He gave a quick glance at the indigo sky. "My, my," he said, "how could I be running so late? I nearly forgot my shoes while dressing, and now I might miss the start of the ball. Please, let us walk down together." The baron held his arm out to her, ready to sweep her swiftly away.

Swallowing the impulse to say, *No, thank you, I would rather stay behind and search the aviary after you leave,* Olga gave her best impression of a smile and turned to walk alongside him as he led her back toward the ballroom. She wasn't sure, but she thought she saw him steal a glance at his bevy of swans, which had formed a single-file line out of the aviary and begun moving toward the lake.

Another somber cry emerged from the forest, riding an errant gust of wind, as if hopeful that someone might answer at last.

nine

As Baron Sokolov steered Olga into the ballroom, music had already begun to play. The twang of strings and trill of flutes jangled with the steps and claps of the first set of dancers. The room was warm, even though the doors leading to the garden had been opened. A dense perfume of honey and sage filled the air.

Olga was eager to return to the aviary, but she also wanted to find Pavel, so she swallowed her impatience and circled the room. A steady stream of guests poured through the open doors, forming pairs while they awaited the start of the next dance.

As the couples gathered and servants approached with trays of canapés, Olga discovered Pavel outside the ballroom in the cool air of the garden. A haze of golden light spilled through the open doors onto the pebbled path.

Pavel was seated on a bench next to the young woman Anna. She was lovely in the twilight, her sea-green dress gracefully arranged as though she were the subject of a painting.

"Olga! Have you met Anna?" Pavel exclaimed as she approached.

"It is so delightful to meet you again," said Anna. Each word that passed between her lips spun and twirled through the air, and she bounced on her seat a little as she spoke. "Pavel speaks so highly of you. It sounds like the two of you have been on so many adventures together—I would love to hear more. I've read stories where people are chased by bandits and fight villainous foes. To meet people who have actually done such things is thrilling!"

"It's not much fun when you're dodging arrows," Olga said gruffly, and the delight fell from Anna's face. The young woman flushed with embarrassment as if she had just spilled punch on herself.

"You're being rude," said Pavel softly.

Olga wasn't used to the annoyance in his voice.

"I agree," Pauk hissed from Olga's pocket. "She seems nice."

"Hello-lovely-to-see-you-again-too-hope-you're-having-a-pleasant-evening," Olga said to Anna with forced cheer. Then she sighed and said, "I'm sorry, I'm just in need of Pavel's assistance." She turned her attention to her friend. "I have something to show you."

Pavel stood, and Olga spun on her heel, ready to zip back to the aviary, but instead, he pushed down on her shoulders, forcing her to fill the spot he had just vacated.

"You need to meet people other than the ones you plan to steal from," he said in a low voice. Then he declared, "I shall bring you both some refreshments!"

Glaring at his retreating form, Olga hardly heard the question Anna asked her.

"I was just wondering if you enjoy stories as much as Pavel," said Anna. "Or music? Music is like poetry; it seems to capture the feelings of things so perfectly. Do you have a favorite poem? Or a favorite story? Even just a favorite word—I love the word *persimmon*." Any agitation Anna felt at Olga's churlishness had been swept away, and her conversation was now a stream of ever-flowing enthusiasm.

Poems were certainly not of interest to Olga. The idea of reading something all about *feelings* had never seemed much fun; but she knew that Pavel—and apparently Pauk, for that matter—would consider it rude if she actually said that. So instead, she simply replied, "Do you? Have a favorite story?"

"Oh yes! I have many favorites," Anna said, and her soft smile returned. "Fairy tales especially. They make me believe in love and hope and magic. I wish I could meet an evil witch, or break a curse—it would be so thrilling, don't you think?" Anna seemed capable of talking without stopping for breath.

Olga had to bite in a groan. This was far more chatting than she enjoyed. But across the room she spotted Pavel, who gave an exaggerated smile and mimed that Olga should keep the conversation flowing. "And what's your favorite fairy tale?" asked Olga in spite of herself.

"There's one about a girl who goes to a ball and falls in love with a prince," said Anna. "A bit like this ball, don't you think?! I'd never been to a ball before coming here, but I've always imagined what they would be like. Do you like to imagine your perfect life? I've struggled to decide whether I would rather be a tsaritsa of unearthly beauty with hair like a raven's wing, or a warrior queen riding my mare into battle with honor guiding my sword."

Had she been feeling generous, Olga might have asked what it was that intrigued Anna about that particular story— whether it was the romance or something else. If Anna, like Olga, sometimes felt trapped in her life and wanted to find a way out—a new way of living. Maybe it was something they shared, this feeling of wanting to make their own choices.

Instead, Olga thought only of how silly it was that Anna liked stories that were meant for little kids, stories that were nothing more than fantasy. Nothing good could come out of believing such nonsense. "My mother used to tell me fairy tales. The ones with happy endings."

"Used to? Why did she stop?" asked Anna, as if the idea of someone no longer telling such stories were a subject of true horror.

"She died."

There was a heavy silence before Anna replied, "I'm so sorry."

Olga gritted her teeth, wishing she had held her tongue. When she was small, Olga had cried herself to sleep, wondering if her magic could have saved her mother. But she hadn't known how to use magic at all then. Even what little she knew now would not have been enough to change her mother's fate. Instead, Olga had had to save herself, to find food and shelter, to work each day to get by, and it had required so much of her that she'd had no time to dwell on sorrow.

Perhaps that was why she disliked stories so much. In stories, orphans and urchins and servants and cursed children always got a happily ever after. But Olga knew there was no such thing. Life went on: new challenges, new people, new discoveries, new disappointment.

The truth was, her mother had died and her father wanted nothing to do with her. There was no happy ending. And when Mr. Bulgakov had found her and taken her in, he had confirmed what she already knew: that in the end, she had to look after herself.

Anna's expression suddenly brightened, a ray of sunshine slicing through a gray cloud. Olga turned to find Pavel approaching, one hand balancing a tray stacked with honey cakes. They were Pavel's favorite, Olga knew, fluffy and sweet. The other hand somehow held three drinks. He handed one to Olga, who set it on the bench untouched.

"I still need to show you something," Olga said, pivoting to Anna to add, "You don't mind, do you?"

"I was hoping Anna might join me for a dance," Pavel interjected.

But Anna shook her head. "I'm afraid I've hurt my ankle. I'm happy here with a book, I promise! You should go." She pulled a small book out of her reticule and made a show of opening it.

There was little argument Pavel could make now that Anna had said she didn't want to dance. Keeping half an eye on Baron Sokolov, Olga marshaled Pavel to the far side of the room, where they were able to slip through the doors.

"Excuse me!" called a voice.

Olga flinched. Sneaking around unnoticed was a skill she usually excelled at. She turned to find one of the twin boys holding something out to her.

"You dropped this," he said. He handed her a spool of thread that must have fallen out of her satchel.

"Thank you," she said, taking it from him.

The boy gave a small bow and returned to his brother. Olga watched them for a moment as they raced back to a table laden with cakes. She was suddenly struck with the thought that it would be fun to run and play with them in the ballroom. But she shook her head, rejecting the notion.

As she steered Pavel toward the entrance hall, he too seemed distracted, glancing behind them at the ballroom.

Olga pinched her lips. "We need to follow the strand I found while it's fresh."

"But—" Pavel began. He bounced on the balls of his feet.

"You want to return to the ball, don't you?"

"Don't you?" he said.

"I want to find the Scarlet Heart. And that means looking in the aviary."

Pavel let out an extravagant groan, but he followed her.

Olga kept her eyes resolutely forward, forcing herself to ignore the jaunty music and the scents of sugar and roses as she led Pavel away.

When they entered the aviary, it was exactly as Olga had hoped: quiet and empty. Baron Sokolov was not here, and many of the birds were roosting in nests or tucked behind rocks. The only sound was the faint hooting of owls in the nearby forest. And the strand of magic was gone.

A grunt of frustration escaped her. If they'd been faster, they might not have lost its trail. But at least she now had a starting place. There was something special about this aviary. . . .

Inside her pocket, Pauk squirmed again.

"The birds are asleep," Olga hissed at him. "They won't eat you."

"What? Eat who?" asked Pavel.

"Nothing!" said Olga. She ought to tell him that she'd

found someone who could help them in their search of the palace, but Pavel was not going to react well to that someone having eight hairy legs.

Pulling a small strand of her own magic to act as a lantern, Olga began to search the space. They checked stones, searched for knotholes in the branches, but found nothing.

"Maybe there's something in the birds' nests?" Pavel suggested. "Anna told me a story of a bird that stored jewels in its nest amongst its eggs."

"That's just a story," said Olga. "A flight of fancy."

Pavel laughed. "Did you do that on purpose?"

"Do what?"

"Make a joke. Saying *flight of fancy* when we're talking about birds."

"I don't make jokes," said Olga.

"Sure you do. Just not always on purpose."

Olga shook her head, ignoring him, and began climbing branches to check the nests, just in case, teasing apart twigs and lifting dry grass. There were at least a dozen nests that she could find, and they were all empty.

Grinding her teeth, Olga finally had to admit defeat. She dropped from a tree branch, her palms red from climbing and her cheeks flushed from frustration. But her resolve wasn't shaken. They might not have found anything yet, but that didn't mean the aviary was a dead end. They just had to search harder.

"We'll come back tomorrow," she said with forced cheer. "I can tell we're getting closer."

ten

B ut Pavel was late to meet Olga the following day as the clock struck noon. He had returned to the ball after their search, and Olga regretted that she hadn't forced him to retreat to his room so that he could rise early, as she had done.

After waiting more than an hour, she arrived at Pavel's room to find him sprawled across the large bed, still asleep. He hadn't even managed to cover himself with one of the silk blankets, and he was still wearing the clothes he'd donned for the ball the night before, a deep red velvet that clashed with his hair and made him look like some sort of fire serpent.

"You're late," she said, stomping into the room, purposefully making as much noise as she could until she was standing next to his bed.

Pavel rolled over and groaned. "Five more minutes," he said.

Olga frowned. He could sleep through an earthquake, probably even a volcanic eruption. She wanted to pull him up and

drag him onto the floor by the foot, but he was much bigger than her. He'd be difficult to move unless he was willing.

But Olga had a few tricks up her sleeve. She grabbed the silken bedcover and yanked.

Pavel only rolled across the bed, still fast asleep.

"Fire!" she shouted. Still Pavel didn't budge.

She had one final trick. Opening her pocket, Olga peered down at Pauk. The spider appeared to be snoozing, his legs curled under him, snoring faintly. She hissed and Pauk woke with a jolt.

"What?!" he snapped. "I was sleeping."

"I don't know how you expect to search the palace if you're asleep half the time."

He grumbled but didn't disagree.

"We need to wake Pavel too," Olga added. She leaned close to the spider and whispered her idea.

Pauk grunted his assent, still grumpy at being awoken. With careful fingers, Olga plucked the spider from her pocket. She stretched her arm out over Pavel's sleeping form, and then the spider descended on a strand of silk. Pauk hovered just above Pavel's nose. Extending a long leg, Pauk gave the nose a flick.

When Pavel didn't move, Pauk swung closer. Landing on Pavel's forehead, the spider began to dance, intruding on Pavel's slumber with tap-tapping tiny feet.

After a second there was a shriek, and Olga pulled Pauk to safety while Pavel wrestled with the blankets and pillows. "I'm up, I'm up!" he said.

"Good," Olga said with a smirk. "Now we go back to the aviary." She dashed toward the wardrobe and grabbed a shirt and trousers, tossing them in his direction before searching the room for his boots.

"Can't we search somewhere else?" asked Pauk. "I don't want to go back there." His long legs twitched as he cowered.

"We both saw the strand there. You know that's where we need to keep searching," Olga answered.

"But it's daytime," the spider whined. "The birds will be back. Can't I just stay here with him?" He bobbed his little hairy body in Pavel's direction.

"He's coming with me," said Olga.

"Are you sure?"

Olga was about to ask what Pauk meant, but she turned to find that Pavel had already fallen asleep again. He was back to his starfish sprawl across the bed. "Ugh! Fine! Stay here with him. But if he wakes up again, make sure to hide, or he'll try to squish you."

"I don't mind *him*," said Pauk. He nestled atop a discarded pillow, curling up for sleep. "It's birds that I hate."

Throwing her hands in the air, Olga left both of them behind in the room, determined to follow the magic, Pavel or no Pavel.

Daylight meant that the aviary was once again aflutter with activity. Birds warbled and swooped low over Olga's head, forcing her to duck. Every tree in the aviary hid a hundred nooks and crannies. Olga tugged at her boots, prepared to climb tree boughs, peel away bark, dig through bird droppings. She'd pry up the stones paving the paths if she had to.

But the echo of footsteps made her dart behind a small section of fencing, and she had just managed to conceal herself when the baron entered the space. She peered between the leaves, watching as he took a seat and withdrew a pipe from the pocket of his jacket, then leaned back to puff on it in silence.

He was directly between her and the corridor back to the entrance hall. She studied her surroundings. There was another door, which was closer but would still be difficult to reach unnoticed, plus the gate that led outside to the forest. In a low squat, Olga inched toward the gate, holding her breath so as not to make a sound. She tugged on it gently to avoid making it creak. It was locked.

Stifling a groan, Olga returned to her hiding place. It looked like she would have to wait until the baron was gone. But this might be a good chance to watch and see if his actions revealed anything useful. She tucked her legs under her, prepared to wait as long as was necessary.

He sat in silence, puffing on his pipe and admiring his birds.

She must have been dozing when the baron's voice woke her. Heart pounding, she bit down a yelp, grateful to realize that he was talking to someone else, not her. There was no way to tell how long they'd both been there, except that the shadows stretched long over the ground.

"The spell will only work if it includes something she loves," he muttered. "She loved music, and dancing. And she loved swans most of all. What more can I do?"

There was no one else in the aviary with him. Who was he talking to?

"But she's close, I can feel it."

Olga's heart was pounding in her ears. Did he know she was hiding in the aviary? She looked back toward the gate, wondering if it could be forced open without attracting the baron's notice. Unlikely.

"Once she's returned, we can finish what we started."

At this, Olga exhaled. He wasn't talking about her after all.

There was a gentle rustle, and through the hedge Olga spotted a cluster of swans gathered near the baron's chair. She had to hold in a laugh. He was talking to the swans!

The swans didn't reply, and Olga found herself wondering if the baron had lost touch with reality. He continued muttering to them, until with a jolt of surprise he noticed the time and rushed to stand. "It's nearly sunset," he said, tapping his watch as if the swans could read it. Swiftly he left through the passage toward the ballroom, and Olga felt her stomach relax. She stood, her legs aching.

Olga approached the swans with careful steps, not wanting to frighten them while she poked around for signs of magic.

One of the swans was clearly the creature Pavel had rescued yesterday. There were still bloodstains on its wings and legs, but it didn't seem sick or distressed. In fact, it inched closer to Olga as she approached, curiosity lighting its dark eyes.

"I found a strand of magic here before. Do you know where it was leading?" Olga asked, recalling how the baron had spoken to them.

As if in answer, the injured swan separated from the others and began waddling toward a door Olga hadn't noticed before.

"You—you didn't understand me, did you?"

With its long, slender neck, the swan leaned forward and nipped at her legs.

"Okay!" she shouted, jumping out of the way. "What, you want me to go in there?"

The swan turned and waddled again toward the door. It stopped before entering, watching Olga until she passed through the dark opening. The swan did not follow.

Olga found herself in an unfamiliar corridor that ended on a lone door. The air had grown thicker somehow, like she was

underwater. She plunged forward, the eerie quiet pressing against her ears.

She reached for the iron handle. As her fingers brushed the metal, Olga felt a shock of energy that knocked her backward.

Her hand and wrist throbbed. She crouched for a moment, breathless, cradling her hand to her chest.

What was that?

She stepped forward cautiously, this time stopping her hand just short of the door. The air was warm around the handle, and a tingle ran up her spine. Her neck itched.

Magic. Whatever was behind the door, she had no doubt there was magic in it. Strings of magic gathered around the door like cobwebs. She pressed a fingertip into the tangle and twirled it—magic buzzed around her finger.

It took her breath away.

Olga tested the handle, reaching slowly, waiting for a second shock that never arrived. It was locked.

Something clattered nearby, something like footsteps. Olga darted back the way she'd come. She wanted to find Pavel, to tell him what she'd found. That door had to be hiding something important—Olga knew it.

She reentered the aviary, ready to thank the swan for its help, but it was gone. All the swans seemed to have disappeared. An owl hooted overhead. Frogs croaked. But the aviary appeared empty . . . except for a solitary figure who stood in the middle of the path.

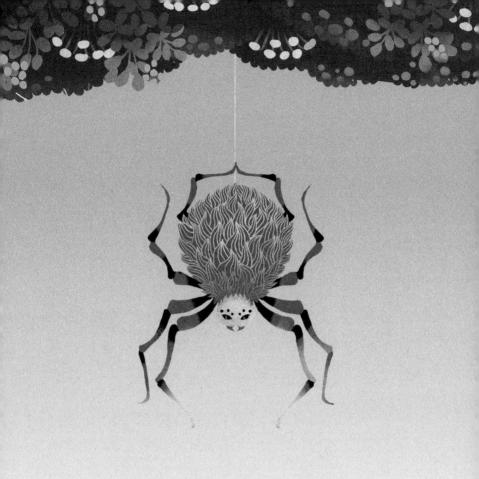

The Spider Spins
His Fourth Tale

I wish to tell you now, little ones, of a young man who grew up in a small village. When his parents died of a sudden illness, it was the villagers who raised him, giving him work, food, and a bed to sleep in. He assisted on a nearby farm, and though it was difficult work, it was honest, and he grew strong in body and mind. He had dreams of being a bogatyr—a knight who protected others as his village had protected him.

One day the dust of the road stirred under a horse's hooves, and a bogatyr in full armor entered the village square. Seeing the boy's strength and resilience, the bogatyr offered to take him on as a squire. The boy was delighted. So eager was he to accept, he waved off the counsel of the village elders—who could have told him that the knight was not an honest or trustworthy man.

It was not until the boy had left the village that he discovered the man was not a bogatyr at all, but had merely pretended, to trick the villagers. How disheartening! Still, the man was able to teach him about weapons and fighting. The boy was now not only strong but skilled in combat.

And so he grew up on the road, always traveling from town to town. The man earned their food and shelter through stealing and swindling—not the honest work that the boy had hoped for.

Often he wished to return to his village, regretting the dreams that had encouraged him to leave.

Together they traveled the countryside, and many years had passed when they entered a small village.

The village had just buried a young mother who had left a daughter all alone. The little girl had no other family, and the villagers were searching for someone who could help her.

The boy saw his chance to do what he had always hoped he could as a bogatyr: to protect those who needed him, to stay loyal and true. He begged his master to let the girl join them in their travels, and when his master agreed, the girl looked at the boy with such relief that his heart swelled. Though the boy was not a knight, he had done a good deed, something a bogatyr would have done.

So I ask you, little ones: did his wish come true?

eleven

Baron Sokolov was in the center of the aviary, well-dressed and rosy-cheeked, and he turned as Olga entered.

"My dear, what a pleasant surprise!" He spoke in a cheery tone, but his gaze flicked between Olga and the corridor she had just left. Olga had the feeling of being inspected, like he was checking her seams and stitching to find snags or bits that had begun to unravel.

She tried to wrap herself in the costume of someone who had a perfectly good explanation. "I heard one of the swans crying and worried it might be hurt." It was very near to the truth. She *had* heard an injured swan yesterday.

"That's very thoughtful!" he said. But his tone became more serious as he continued, "Though I'm not sure if I believe you."

The baron took a step closer. In the dim light, she could see that something looked different about him. It took a moment for Olga to realize that she could see the glitter of magic strands around him. He was clothed in the same magic the swan had been.

She suddenly wished she hadn't come here without Pavel or Pauk. Her heart pattered like rain on a barn roof. "What do you—" Olga began, but Baron Sokolov held up a hand to silence her.

"The others who come to this valley join the revelry without question, just as your friend has," he said delicately. "But you—you've been searching for something."

Olga's mind raced. But before she could reply, Baron Sokolov answered his own question:

"Can you see the strands?"

Olga stared at him in surprise. He knew. Not just that the magic was here, surrounding him, surrounding this valley, but that Olga could see it and feel it too.

Baron Sokolov chuckled and stepped closer. "I have been needing someone who can work heartstrings, and now here you are. . . ."

Nervousness had shifted to curiosity amidst Olga's surprise at his words. He wanted someone with magic?

She could use this to her advantage.

"What is it you want?" she asked.

The baron regarded her. With long strides, he approached the corridor behind Olga, and as he stepped through a sliver of moonlight, Olga noticed something. The strands of magic surrounding him were fraying. A few patches, one on his cheek, another on his shoulder. And beneath the strands of magic was something jagged and gray, like lizard skin. As he moved, she thought she glimpsed scales. Olga wondered how she had missed noticing before.

The baron paused in the moonlight, and a sneer eclipsed his face. The expression made Olga feel unsteady. "What I want," he said, "is your friend's heartstring."

Olga was suddenly breathless. "Pavel?" she asked. Pavel, who had never done anything to harm anyone, whose greatest crime was getting distracted by flowers and forgetting his belongings.

Mr. Bulgakov's words thrummed in Olga's memory, conjuring images of an evil spirit with an endless hunger, of people who had disappeared. Olga now understood with bone-deep certainty that this spirit was hiding inside the baron, speaking to her. It wanted to take Pavel into its clutches, and she had led him here. Eager, helpful, wide-eyed Pavel.

"But what use is Pavel's heartstring to you?" said Olga. "You can't use someone else's strand for your magic."

Baron Sokolov chuckled. "Oh, can I not?"

The man waved his hand with a flourish, beckoning, and a strand of magic slithered toward her. Before she could react, it had coiled and knotted around her ankles. Her heart drummed a frantic rhythm. Fear squeezed her throat. Without intending to move her feet, Olga was compelled to march like a marionette down the passageway until they reached the door at the end of the darkened corridor.

Olga could still see the strands of magic vibrating around the lock and handle, could feel the heat of the shock it had given her before. Baron Sokolov reached into the pulsating tangle, and the threads seemed to recognize him, unfurling until the lock stood bare. Then he turned the handle and the door creaked open.

It filled Olga with a strange excitement, like she was being let in on a secret. And yet that feeling was soon replaced by an aching dread, for she knew that no one would ever be able to find her if things went wrong. Why had she come *alone*?

Their footsteps echoed as they stepped inside a circular room. Bright green light made Olga squint. The room was filled with shelves laden with vials and jars. Stacks of books covered the floors. A desk was barely visible under a mountain of papers.

In the middle of the room stood a stone bowl as tall as Olga's chest. Water filled it to its brim. The rippling surface glowed green, painting wriggling patterns on the room's mossy walls.

Olga felt herself stagger, and she realized that he had released the magical binding from around her feet.

The baron turned to face her, his features eerie in the strange green light. "Long ago, I lost something very precious to me," he said.

Olga listened with rapt attention to his every word. Was it possible he was about to tell her about the Scarlet Heart? Had it been stolen from him already?

"My wife disappeared. Along with our unborn child."

Olga deflated a little.

"It was the most horrific experience of my life, to discover her bed empty, to be haunted by worries of my beloved. But she left something behind, a spell that kept me from following her, and revealed that leaving had been her *choice*." His hand bunched into a fist, and he slammed it against the stone wall. A growl escaped him. "I swore I would bring her back and *show* her the love I have for her. Do you know how?" His glistening eyes met Olga's.

She remembered his words from earlier, when she'd been eavesdropping. "The balls. The swans. The flowers. Everything?"

"Everything." He nodded with that familiar twisted smile. He seemed exceedingly pleased with himself. "There are great tendrils of magic spreading out from this valley, searching for her. When they return her to me, she will find a home that reminds her of how happy she was once upon a time."

Olga imagined a spider at the center of an enormous web, and she wondered if his wife was like the fly that didn't want to be caught.

The baron continued. "But my magic could not reach her. I waited, knowing that if I ever wanted to see her again, I had to find a way to expand my search, to stretch my magic farther. And while I waited, the answer came to me."

He paused for a moment, as if giving Olga time to guess. When she didn't answer, he went on. "People had started to come to the palace, drawn in by my spell. Stories began to spread about this valley. Some said it was deserted, cursed, a place to steer clear of. But others said it promised your heart's desire—a place where wishes were granted."

"I saw the spell. I felt it," Olga said in realization. She wanted to kick herself for giving in to its pull. Pavel couldn't see the magic, but she could, and still she'd insisted on coming here.

"In my years of studying magic, I had discovered how to use the heartstrings of others to grow my own powers." He gestured at the books and papers surrounding them. "The people drawn here: they were the answer. So I made this palace into a place where their dreams came true. Whether they longed for love or beauty, joy or admiration, their wishes were granted to them by magic for as long as they stayed here. And the longer they stayed here, the better they served my needs. The strongest magic comes from a full heart."

But the halls had been so quiet during the day, the palace seemingly empty once the balls ended. "What happens to them when you use their heartstrings?" Olga asked warily. "Does it kill them?"

"Good heavens no, you dramatic child!" He laughed, and the sound echoed in the small space. "But it does make them . . . less like themselves. They need rest during the day, so they can enjoy themselves at night."

"I won't let you touch Pavel," she said, not fully believing his answer.

The baron peered at her, giving her a look she hated. It was the expression adults had sometimes when they thought her too childish or naive. "My guests want to be here, and so does your friend. You've seen the way the balls captivate him. He wants something that he can only find here. His heart is open, and without realizing it, he is offering his heartstring readily. It would be so easy for me to take it, to weave it into my spells. And once I did that, he would refuse to leave. You could drag him out, and he would return. He would be tied here, just like the others."

Olga's jaw had begun to hurt, and she realized she'd been clenching it. Part of her wondered if there was some way to escape, if she could use her magic to buy enough time for her to find Pavel and run away into the forest. But that would mean giving up any hope of the Scarlet Heart.

The injustice of it all burned inside her. She didn't want to be trapped here, but she didn't want to return to her old life either.

She wanted to make a new life for herself. She wanted the jewel she had come for.

"Then what is it you want from me?" she asked, failing to hide the resentment in her voice.

"Come to the water," said Baron Sokolov, motioning to the stone bowl in the center of the room. Its green light continued to dance and dab strokes of light over the stone walls. "And tell me what you see."

Olga approached the bowl and peered down. Baron Sokolov's reflection watched her, but instead of the face of a man, Olga saw what she had glimpsed in the shadows of the aviary: Bits of his flesh were worn away, revealing that rotten core. Slimy skin and

spiked gray scales. She was seeing the real face of Baron Sokolov, not the one that was decorated with magic.

"What's happening to you?" she asked, trying to hide her disgust.

"Searching for my wife while maintaining the illusions in the ballroom has been too much. The magic began to draw from other parts of me, destroying me little by little." His hand hovered over his cheek, where the strange scales were visible. "The greater my power grows, the faster the magic unravels. One day the spell will collapse, and all will be lost." He looked at Olga, his blue eyes full of electric energy. "But then you came here, drawn by the magic as all others have been. And you are exactly what I need."

Olga could hear the desperation in him, and she realized she'd witnessed this before. She'd watched Mr. Bulgakov bargain with people and use their needs to his advantage. Olga knew the routine, the speeches, remembered the cool resolve Mr. Bulgakov always used, like a cardplayer concealing his hand. It was an opportunity. The baron needed her magic.

"What do you expect me to do?" Olga asked. She fought to keep her tone cool, though she was sure he could hear her heart pounding.

"Repair my spells. Throughout the valley the threads have begun to fray, but with your magic skills, you can restore them."

Such a deal would mean helping Baron Sokolov in tricking and trapping future people. More would come to the valley, used by the baron for his own purposes, and it would be thanks to her.

Olga also realized that her magic wasn't strong enough

to perform such a task. Even if she could do it without fainting, she had never used her magic for something so large before. She could barely manage simple illusions. Somehow she would have to trick him into thinking she was capable of such magic and do enough to keep him from becoming suspicious. But if she *could* manage it, what more might he be willing to offer her?

It was another thing Mr. Bulgakov had taught her. In any bargain, there was always a third option, a way to get the upper hand that no one suspected.

She quelled her nerves, only her toes betraying her anxiety by wiggling inside her boots. "Without my help, you'll lose your grip on your magic. Letting us walk free isn't enough."

At this, the baron did show his surprise. His white eyebrows twitched; his lips tightened. And she saw a flicker, for only a second, of true fear. If she didn't do what he asked, his search for his family would collapse around him.

The feeling thrilled her. She loved this dance, this game of trying to be one step ahead. And with the baron, she was winning.

"What is it you want?" he asked. "To be a graceful dancer, an athlete, a champion? To best a rival? To have the admiration of the tsardom?"

"I want the jewel. The Scarlet Heart."

"Ah," he said. "Riches. How predictable."

This cut did hit its mark, and Olga couldn't help but ask, "What do you mean?"

"I've told you, everyone who comes to this valley is searching for something. But people are less unique than they like to believe. They all want the same things: wealth, beauty, power. I should have known you were no different."

"And what of it?" Olga said. "The treasure means things for me. It means I can have a different life. And Pavel too."

"Does it?" he said. Gone was the congenial baron she had known in the ballroom; this man before her was cool and shrewd. "Perhaps you're not as capable with your magic as I thought, if you need a paltry jewel to secure your future."

"If you can offer me the Scarlet Heart, then I will use my magic to repair your spells." Olga fought to sound confident. She would find a way to do this. She had a path to the jewel now, and she was going to take it.

The baron thought for a moment, and again there was that trace of desperation in his gaze. "Done," he answered at last.

He extended his hand to her and she shook it, trying not to squirm at his slick, cold touch. He grasped her hand, pulling her closer as he said in a slithering voice, "You're bound to this bargain now." He let her go, and with a backward step vowed, "If you attempt to cheat me, you will regret it."

twelve

The next morning Olga awoke to find Pauk on her pillow. His eyes glittered as he watched Olga put on her cloak and relace her boots. Olga knew he was waiting for her to speak, but she struggled to find the words. The bargain she'd made with the baron still felt more like a fever dream, visions and snippets of half-remembered phrases, than a real conversation she'd shared.

"Do I want to know what you found?" he asked at last.

It was tempting to avoid telling Pauk anything. But he had helped her, and it would be fulfilling their bargain to confirm that the baron was at the center of the magic in the valley.

Olga also knew she could never reveal to Pavel the bargain she'd just made. If she told him, he'd want to rescue everyone. And when he did, the baron would know, and her bargain with him would be void. All chances of finding the Scarlet Heart would be gone.

With a sigh, Olga explained the bargain she had made. She waited for the spider to plead with her not to go through with it—but instead, Pauk looked thoughtful. "I'll go with you, then. You might need my help."

"But I'm helping the baron. Are you supposed to object? Shouldn't you try to stop me?"

"That's for my queen to decide. For now, I'd rather not let something happen to you."

Olga wasn't sure how helpful the spider could be, but she opened her pocket in invitation. He deftly slipped inside.

Together they made their way first to the breakfast room. The food held far less appeal now that Olga knew it was enchanted, and she swallowed without savoring anything as though forced to eat sawdust. Between bites, she slipped biscuits and pastries into her satchel, preparing for the long day ahead.

She trudged through the palace gardens toward the gate. Olga couldn't help but feel annoyed at all the illusions she'd overlooked since her arrival. Everything she'd seen in the palace—the honey cakes, the entrancing music, the swirl of color and laughter—none of it had been real. These people had been bewitched by the baron to believe in a fairy tale. And now she was in on it.

OooEEEaaaooo. The familiar low moan greeted her as she approached the forest. There was something about this place that the baron still wasn't telling her. A worry snatched at her mind that he'd trick her to get the better end of their bargain. She needed to stay a step ahead of him, to uncover what he was hiding. Going into the forest to repair his magic was also a chance to discover what was lurking in the shadows.

It was slow moving, trying to make her way over roots and between the trees. But she trekked on, searching for the tug she had first felt when looking out over the valley and following the feeling.

A glimmer of light winked in the distance, and she followed it to find the elusive strand. It seemed to wiggle and hum at her touch. Behind her it trailed back toward the palace, and ahead of her it stretched up the slopes of the hill. This was a more powerful magic than she'd ever encountered, and it sent a tremor down her spine. The baron's strands weren't simply illusions—they held real power, dangerous and unpredictable.

The baron had instructed her to follow the length of the strand, searching for the weak spots where the magic was fraying. She made her way up the slope, the strand leading her over moss-covered rocks and through prickly bushes. She slipped, and that strange low moan continued to hum on the wind.

At last, she found an instance of what the baron had described. There was a patch where the strand had begun to unravel. When she touched it, it writhed in her hand like a living thing, and she could feel the disease that had taken hold of it.

Olga wondered what the baron expected. Was she supposed to replace the thread entirely with her own magic? She searched for the gap. The length of damaged thread spanned more than fifteen feet. She could feel where the threads were fraying and where they were whole again on the other side. She couldn't possibly replace this with nothing but her own magic.

Pauk spoke quietly, startling her. "Does something worry you?" he asked. Olga could feel the weight and presence of the spider as he climbed out of her pocket. There was a comfort in having Pauk nearby.

"I'm not sure how I'll be able to fix this. . . . The baron has asked me to make repairs, but there's too much magic needed. If I fainted here in the forest . . ."

The spider climbed onto the magic thread in her hands, touching the edge of the decay. "You have the power to do as the baron asks," he said.

"How could you know that?" Olga asked.

"Human magic came from spiders. It's our silk that you carry around your hearts," said Pauk. When Olga's eyes widened, he continued, "Don't you know the story of the spider queen's gift? It's been passed down for thousands of spider generations." He huffed a little, though Olga could tell he wasn't actually offended.

"Stories . . . ," said Olga. "You mean to tell me you share silly fairy tales too?"

"What are stories but truth in a fine gown?" chirped Pauk.

"What do you mean?"

"At the heart of every great story is something true. No one would tell it otherwise. The tellings simply look different— they're dressed to appeal to the listener."

Olga shook her head. "Stories are make-believe. Just a tool to get people to listen, or believe in something. Like an illusion." She remembered all the ways she'd used her magic for Mr. Bulgakov, wincing at the memory of the girl in the market and the music box. The baron was doing the same to his guests. "Just like magic. It's creating lies."

"Sometimes," said the spider. "It wasn't always that way. The first magic was motivated by the deepest love of the human heart. But humans have a tendency to distort what they need into something they want. And when that happens, nothing is ever enough."

There was a long silence as Olga tried to untangle the spider's meaning. It made her brain hurt. At last she said, "So we pull magic from our hearts"—a smile started to twitch on her lips—"and you pull magic from your . . . ?"

"Don't be rude," said the spider. Pauk instead directed his attention back to the thread, examining it with his long legs. Or—Olga supposed—his hands. She'd never really thought about whether spiders had hands or not.

"In the old days, humans used only little bits of their magic. They didn't need more, because they would attach the magic to something real," Pauk said thoughtfully.

"I already know how to do that. I tied illusions to jewelry and music boxes—"

"No, no," said Pauk. "This isn't wrapping magic *around* an object, it's *making* something with magic. It's why people have always had magic smelted into swords or gold chains, cemented within the stones of a house for protection, poured into the quicksilver of a looking glass. The magic seeps into what's being made, and the object becomes fully magical, even if the strand that was planted was very small."

Olga rubbed her head with the heels of her hands. "I don't know how to make a sword. I can barely even stitch together a dress!"

"You can sew?"

"Poorly!"

"Do you have thread with you?"

Olga touched her satchel. "Yes," she said.

"This could work," said the spider. "Let me show you."

The spider's deft legs took hold of the thread Olga offered. "Now, I need a pinch of your heartstring. May I?" At Olga's nod, Pauk's little spider leg touched Olga's chest and withdrew a small strand of magic. In wonder Olga watched as the spider twisted the thread and the pinch of magic together. As he did, the thread began to shimmer and crackle, dancing with an internal energy. It was alive with power, as if it could pull the very sun across the sky.

Olga touched the strand. It felt nothing like regular thread, but it was different from her raw heartstring too—it had become something new, something that was both things and neither of them. Pauk pulled the magic strand across the gap in the baron's magic, tying it on both ends. It pulsed with a new power, healthier than the baron's decaying strand.

"Now you try."

"I still don't understand," said Olga. "If this is wicked magic, why are you helping me fix it? Shouldn't you be trying to destroy it? Isn't that why you came to the palace?"

"I suppose," said Pauk, "it's because I don't wish to merely destroy what's wicked. I think we need to change it to something good. And I can help you learn how to do that."

Olga wasn't sure if she understood or agreed, but she didn't argue either. Pauk was showing her more about magic than she'd ever learned before.

They followed the strand farther up the slope until they found another place where it had frayed. Olga's fingers weren't nearly as nimble, and she fumbled the braiding, but the magic didn't seem to mind. Olga's magic lengthened and twined around the thread, forging a sturdy rope just like Pauk's. She tied it to the baron's spell.

Olga marveled. "This is incredible," she said, holding the humming strand.

Pauk beamed.

Together they carried on, finding more patches of damaged magic and repairing them. Without Pauk's advice, Olga would have used more magic than she could spend in a single day on the first patch alone. Instead, she so enjoyed the feeling of using her magic in this way that hours passed before she felt the need to stop for a rest.

The trees opened to a glorious vista of the valley below. The lake was smaller and more distant, framed by the mountains all around. She was perhaps halfway up the valley. It would take many hours to make the entire climb.

This was still going to be a difficult task. The valley was enormous, and there had to be a dozen different threads extending like rays from the palace at the center. Even if she spent each day climbing the mountains surrounding them, it would be weeks before she could repair everything.

The sky was a cloudless blue, and she sat down, resting and enjoying the view. A shimmering fog surrounded where she knew the palace to be, and she remembered how easily she too had been drawn into this valley.

"How long have the people been here, do you think?" said Olga.

"According to our stories, it has been many spider

generations," said Pauk. He climbed to sit on Olga's shoulder, his legs catching in the fabric of Olga's shirt. "It's difficult to guess, but I think some of the guests in that palace have been there longer than you've been alive."

"Twelve years of going to balls every night," Olga whispered. "It feels like too much. Aren't they tired? Don't they miss the outside world?"

"I am sure they do. But the baron makes them forget."

"Do you think they'll ever leave?"

"I have hope," said the spider. "I am beginning to suspect our fates are intertwined, and your presence in this valley signals the dawn of change."

The words gripped Olga's heart, pulling her toward a future she felt unprepared to face. She blinked, hoping the spider was wrong. But instead, she simply said, "Then I guess I need to enjoy the cookies while I can."

Olga began her descent toward the lake. Time had slipped away, and she hoped she would be able to return to the palace before night fell.

She liked the way the afternoon sunlight on the leaves painted patterns on the forest floor and made the air shine soft shades of green and gold. At first, she could hear only the sounds of the forest: chirping cicadas, squawking birds, the scuffle of critters in the underbrush.

But there was something else: that ever-present moan on the wind.

Olga tugged her cloak more tightly about her shoulders. Movement at the corner of her vision made her turn, but there was nothing.

And then she saw it: a pale light in the gloom, floating toward her like a feather on the surface of a pond. At first, she thought it was one of the swans. But as it neared, she glimpsed a pointed snakelike face and hooked talons. Heard the threatening rumble of its growl.

It was too close to hide from. Too close to escape.

Then it turned and narrowed its glowing, scarlet eyes. It snarled at her, revealing sharp teeth. Anger contorted its features. The snarl turned into a shriek.

Olga froze, staring at it, hoping that it wouldn't consider her a threat. She slowly held out a hand. "It's okay. I'm not here to hurt you." The words sounded weak and unconvincing, but they were all she had.

The creature shrieked again.

"Olga?" said Pauk, and the spider's voice was quavering. "I think you should run."

Olga had always prided herself on her unwillingness to show fear. She'd been alone, and hungry, and in danger, managing thefts for Mr. Bulgakov and swindling from people who had the power to throw her into a prison to rot. But she had never lost her nerve, never had to fight back tears of worry.

Until today.

Her breaths pulsed. Her chest was tight, like a torrent of fear was raging through, threatening to overflow.

She took a step back, willing her legs to run. And then the creature charged, lurching toward her. Olga turned and fled. She plunged through the forest, tripping over fallen logs, swatting away the thorns and cobwebs that clung to her clothes. Another creature screeched, and it swooped behind her. There had to be somewhere to hide.

"There!" Pauk shouted, and Olga saw it too: an enormous fallen tree near the edge of one of the valley's ravines. Its roots burst from the ground in a tangled mass. She ducked under the trunk, hoping the creatures would get caught among the thick, intersecting roots.

More creatures had gathered now, surrounding the tree,

flooding the grove with their eerie light. Olga yanked off a knotted root with a snap, brandishing it like a sword. One of the animals lurched at her. She slammed the makeshift weapon against the creature's head, knocking it away from her. Another grabbed the root in its jaws and yanked it from her grasp, tossing it aside.

She stared helplessly as the creatures drew near. They began to thrash at the roots of the tree, ripping away Olga's protection, inching closer. . . .

A low rumble sounded, and Olga felt the ground shift beneath her. For a moment she thought the tree was breaking apart. But it was the ravine itself. Rocks began to tumble away, disappearing down the slope below.

The earth shook, and the creatures, spooked by their

nearness to the collapse, retreated, creeping from Olga to lurk in the shadows nearby.

Olga clung to the tree roots until the rumbling stopped. Shivers shook her hands and legs.

She had used too much magic. She could only sit, her eyes closed, hoping she wouldn't lose consciousness here in the middle of the forest.

The figure approached without a sound, and Olga opened her eyes to find a shadow looming over her.

"Can you walk?" asked a voice—an old woman's, it seemed. "You look like you could use a warm fire."

One of the creatures lurking nearby pressed forward. Olga flinched, but the woman held up a hand. "She is not who you seek," she said. "You will not find your revenge here. Now go."

The creatures bowed their heads and obeyed, disappearing between the trees. The tension in Olga's shoulders lessened a little as she watched their retreating forms.

The woman held out a hand to help Olga to her feet. Olga hesitated a moment, and as she did, Pauk skittered up the woman's gown to her shoulder.

Olga expected the woman to flinch, but instead, she chuckled, a low rasping sound. Seeing the trust her spider friend had in this unknown person, Olga realized she was too tired to stay where she was. If the woman had meant any harm, she could have done something while Olga's eyes had been closed.

Slowly, every movement weighted by exhaustion, Olga took the woman's hand. It was warm and . . . hairy. Olga looked up, and light caught the woman's eyes. They glittered, and something seemed odd about them. Then the woman shifted, and another arm moved.

Olga gasped, nearly tumbling backward.

Whoever this woman was—whatever she was—she absolutely was not human. And Olga suspected she knew exactly who had rescued her.

She was in the presence of the spider queen.

thirteen

P art of Olga wanted to back away, but the thought of crawling down the slope while she was still so weak frightened her.

"Who are you?" Olga's voice cracked. She'd lost more strength than she cared to admit.

The reply came low and steady. "Call me Mokosh."

"And . . . *what* are you?"

The woman—queen? spider?—gave a low chuckle. "I once ruled over this valley, long ago." Mokosh moved, and the spider-woman's limbs were jittery, her balance uneven, as though it had been a long time since she'd walked anywhere. "Come— we can talk more where it's warm."

Olga was reluctant to follow this strange woman anywhere, yet she had saved Olga's life and was now offering a place to rest. Perhaps Olga ought to have been frightened. Her legs were shaking. But she felt safe in Mokosh's presence. Slowly, gratefully, Olga nodded.

Together they climbed the slope toward the base of a

craggy cliff. As the trees thinned, Olga could more clearly see the woman's extra arms, extra legs. Skittering movements held a grace and authority—shadow and light seemed to cling to her and form a crown about her angular head. Olga felt the urge to bow.

A section of the cliff's face dipped, and Olga realized they were heading toward a cave. Curtains of webs drooped over the entrance, which the spider queen parted with a sweep of an arm. Firelight flickered from within.

Stooping under the silky canopy, Olga received another shock: Every surface in the cave was covered in spider webs. Webs covered logs to form misshapen chairs. Webs softened the floor of the cave in a glimmering rug. And the spider queen herself, as she turned to face the firelight, was a bewildering mix of human and inhuman. Human-sized, with a human face,

but her movements mimicked those of a spider—all skittering legs and glittering eyes.

"Sit down," Mokosh said, gesturing with an arm. Pauk perched on her hand. And when Olga hesitated, the queen repeated more sternly, "Sit. Rest."

Olga lowered herself into one of the silvery, webby chairs. She expected it to be sticky, but there was only softness. Despite its peculiarity, the cave was warm and comfortable.

Mokosh sat on a throne of fanned tree roots, cushioned with webs. Her gaze was sharp but not unkind. Now that they were in the firelight, her features appeared slightly more human. Curtains of gray hair surrounded a worn face. Brown eyes glowed amber in the light. Her clothes looked like they were woven from the same webs as the furniture, silvery and delicate, draping over her so that it was impossible to tell whether she was angles or curves.

For a moment Mokosh's attention turned away from Olga, and there was an odd series of clicking noises. Following the direction of the spider queen's gaze, Olga realized the sounds came from Pauk, who was communicating to his queen in a spidery language. Mokosh nodded, and her piercing stare was once again on Olga.

"Are you aware of the danger you are in?" Mokosh asked.

The force of the question made Olga shift a little in her seat. What had Pauk told her? "I know of the baron's spells."

"And you saw the creatures lurking in the forest?"

"Yes."

"You could escape, yet you have not."

Olga was beginning to regret coming here. The deal she had made with the baron, and her reasons for it, were none of Mokosh's business. She tried to push herself to stand, but her legs trembled beneath her weight.

"Stay," the spider queen commanded. Then her tone softened a little. "Allow me to tell you a story."

A story wasn't exactly what Olga wanted to hear right now, but she wasn't sure if she had a choice.

The old woman plucked a thread from the webbing of her chair, examining it. She cleared her throat. "Long ago, I gifted a human with a strand of my silk. I was very old, and ready for my eternal rest, and I thought it an act of generosity. You see, the ancient creatures of these mountains all went to sleep long ago. Like them, I am meant to sleep unless a time of great need awakens me." Her amber eyes glittered, and there was a sudden strength to her words, the command of a powerful being. "Recently I awoke to a wretched sound: the valley's cries for help."

Squirming a little, Olga asked, "What? Why?"

"I believe you already know the answer to that question."

Olga did. "Why are you telling me about the valley's cries? What do you expect me to do?"

The spider queen was watching Olga, and Olga had the feeling that Mokosh was trying to see inside her, untwining the knots and tangles of her inner thoughts. Olga drew her knees to her chest, as if they could form a shield.

"I had hoped you might ask how you could help," Mokosh said slowly, deliberately.

"I can't be bothered with other people's concerns," Olga said bitterly. It was what Mr. Bulgakov had always taught her. They had to focus on themselves, on their own survival.

Her words must have angered the spider queen, because a flurry of movement arose around Mokosh. It took Olga a moment to realize that it was a swarm of spiders. Hundreds, no, thousands of them. On the ceiling, the walls, even the old woman's chair. The skittering of many tiny feet against stone echoed through the cave. "I am here to save this valley from the baron's magic," the spider queen said coldly. "He has corrupted my gift. But my own magic has been lost to time. I need your powers."

Need. People were always needing her magic. Mr. Bulgakov, Baron Sokolov, and now Mokosh. Olga touched a hand to her chest, feeling the warm coil of her heartstring. Part of her felt obliged to the spider queen—it was thanks to her that Olga had magic. But none of these worries about the valley felt like Olga's responsibility. "And what if I say no? What if I'd rather leave?"

"Then you'll never find the answers you seek. Your true reason for coming here."

Again, Olga was struck by the strength in Mokosh's voice. There was no mistaking the rumble beneath her words, an ever-present reminder that the spider queen was more powerful than any human.

"What do you mean?" Did Mokosh know about Olga's search for the jewel?

"You won't find the truth about your family."

It was almost as if the ground had split beneath her, and

for a moment Olga wondered if it had. But no, it was only her surprise. No one had mentioned her family for as long as she could remember. Mr. Bulgakov had never asked, and Pavel had kept silent on the subject after Olga told him she didn't want to talk about it back when they first met.

She considered for a moment what Mokosh could possibly reveal about Olga's family, but she stopped herself quickly. "I don't want to know," she said. "I don't need to know someone who never wanted me."

"Do you not? I can see the knot in your own heartstring, a hurt that has stayed with you, always."

Olga's insides twisted. There was an angry part of her that had harbored assumptions that her father knew who she was yet wanted nothing to do with her. That he'd abandoned her and her mother. She'd quelled her fantasies about confronting him, even punishing him. And yet another part had always wished that it was all some mistake, that he'd wanted her after all.

"What would you need me to do?" she asked. She wasn't agreeing to anything. She still had the choice, the chance to say no. But it couldn't hurt to hear what Mokosh wanted.

"I intend to free all the guests of the palace. My subjects have been keeping me informed. . . ." The cloud of spiders surrounding her shifted at her mention of them. "But I need a human with the gift for manipulating heartstrings to complete the spell."

"What would you give me in return if I did?" Olga asked.

Mokosh's expression darkened. "I hope one day you will learn to do right for its own sake and not because of what you will be given in exchange."

The words stung, but Olga wouldn't let her anger show. "I need time to think. Give me until tomorrow."

Spiders skittered on the walls and ceiling while the spider queen considered in silence. "Understood," she said at last.

But the thought of returning to this cave reminded Olga of what had brought her here in the first place, and the memory of those snarling creatures made her heart thump. "How am I supposed to return? What if those creatures find me?"

"I have spoken to them," said Mokosh. "They won't approach you again."

Pauk left Mokosh's chair and crawled up Olga's body to return to her pocket.

The movement brought a warmth to Olga—it felt as though Pauk offered a small amount of protection.

As Olga stood from the chair, Mokosh reached out. The old woman's strange, inhuman hand, with its long angular fingers, wrapped around Olga's wrist. "Be careful, Olga. Playing deadly games yields only deadly rewards."

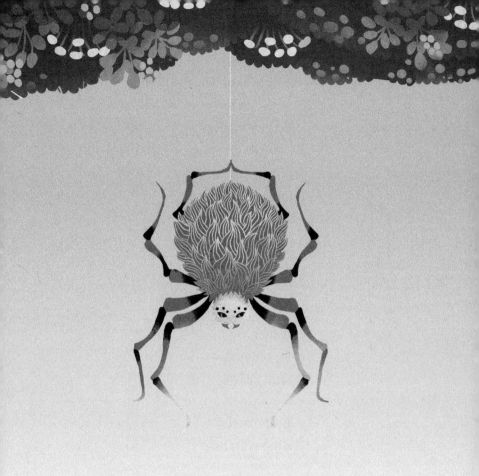

The Spider Spins
His Fifth Tale

My, you are hungry for stories, little ones! Very well, I shall tell you of one who loved stories almost as much as you do. In a village near these mountains, a young woman lost herself in a book. She devoured stories of curious magic, of gallant knights on dangerous adventures, of princes and princesses in star-crossed love.

But that was not her life, of course. She lived in a village at the base of the mountains, where she and her seven sisters worked as seamstresses—very dreary indeed. With each passing season she began to despair of ever going on an adventure akin to the tales she loved—of battling monsters, or enduring curses, or falling in love with a handsome tsarevich. By day she worked with scratchy homespun fabrics (that weren't even made of nettles or frog skin!), and by night she would read until her candle had burned down to nothing, imagining herself in a world very different from this one.

She began to wonder if the dullness of her life was due to how little she resembled the damsels from the stories she loved— the women who were beautiful, and graceful, and unfailingly kind. She wished to be more like them.

But her family had made arrangements for her to marry a man from the village, a man with a terrible temper. He did not like to read at all and told her that she would be expected to put away her childish books when they were wed.

This would not do!

She had heard of a valley not too far from her village where wishes were granted. It was said to lie deep in the mountains, where a lake was surrounded by dense forests swarming with spirits. Only the very bravest were able to reach the lake and their hearts' desire. If she could find the courage, then she could make a wish to become like the heroines in her favorite stories.

And thus, one night she packed her very favorite books and stole away while her sisters were sleeping, to search for her perfect storybook life.

So I ask you, little ones: if she braved treacherous woods and wicked spirits to reach her goal, did she ever truly lack what she longed for?

fourteen

The request from Mokosh had thrown Olga's plans into disarray. Though Olga had denied it in the cave, the old woman had seen a desire that she'd long tried to hide and bury. Something ached inside her, and that ache weighed on her heart as she retreated down the hill, sweating even as the air cooled and night fell.

"Are you going to talk to Pavel?" asked Pauk. The spider was snug in Olga's pocket.

Olga narrowed her eyes. Of course Pauk would want her to tell Pavel everything. She knew what choice Pavel would make—he would choose to save everyone, even if it cost them their chance at the jewel. But Olga wasn't sure. Saving the others was still none of her concern.

"I need to think by myself." She wanted to hole up in her room to consider the spider queen's plans in quiet and solitude.

Yet when she returned to the palace, she found her feet carrying her to the ballroom once more. Even now knowing about the baron's spells, she still struggled to fight their temptation.

The ball had already begun, with the blaring of horns and clapping of hands thumping a feverish rhythm. She ducked past ballroom guests, around the angular man dancing an enthusiastic jig, and past the twin boys. One of the boys looked like he had drunk too much wine—his eyes were glassy, his movements sluggish. His brother teased and jabbed at him. Just as she'd observed with the baron, it seemed the illusions were beginning to crumble, the magic starting to fracture and fray.

Pavel and Anna were once again seated in the garden, their heads bowed close in conversation. Blooming hedges surrounded them, and the water of a nearby fountain danced with splashes of starlight.

They looked up at Olga in surprise as she approached.

Pavel's smile was warm, his voice warmer. "Olga! I'm glad you're here. We have a surprise planned."

The news knocked Olga off-balance. "Now?"

He shook his head, the candlelight flickering in his fiery hair. "Soon." He wore another set of borrowed finery, and the glimmering threads and stiff collar gave him the look of someone who belonged in this world—a true gentleman. The green of his jacket matched his eyes, lush as a forest in summer. He stood and steered Olga by the shoulders onto the bench. "I'll get refreshments." And with that he bounded into the ballroom like a deer in coattails.

Anna's voluminous ball gown rustled as she reached to take Olga's hands. "I was hoping for the chance to speak with you again," said Anna. "Pavel speaks so highly of you—in his stories you're so brave and clever."

The comment took Olga by such surprise that she was speechless for a moment. No one had ever said or thought admiring things about her. Olga was not the hero of one of Anna's beloved ballads—she was no one.

"H-he clearly enjoys spending time with you," Olga managed to say.

"Oh!" said Anna. "Oh no, that can't be true. I'm not very interesting."

With a jolt of surprise at her own compassion, Olga found herself pitying Anna. Something about the baron's spells had drawn Anna here. She had some unfulfilled wish, a hope that kept her trapped here.

Anna continued, not noticing Olga's silence. "But I could tell you a story about something else? One of the ones from my book? I just finished a wonderful epic about a girl who must journey across nine tsardoms to find her lost love: a tsarevich who can transform into a falcon—" She pulled a book from her reticule and began to flip through the pages.

"Why did you come here?" Olga interrupted.

Anna paused, her finger hovering over one of the pages. "My story will be the same as yours, I am sure." She pitched her voice low, like a smuggler delivering stolen secrets.

Olga found herself suddenly worried that Anna too had come here in search of the Scarlet Heart, that Anna was concealing her true intent. "What do you mean?" She tried to keep her voice from shaking.

"The valley offered you something, didn't it? Something you longed for?"

"Yes," said Olga quietly. "They say that everyone who comes here has a wish they hope will be granted. Did you?"

"I . . ." Anna's hands twisted in her lap. But at an encouraging nod from Olga, she spoke. "I wanted something like in a story," she said. "The maidens in tales are always beautiful, charming, elegant, and I was none of those things. I came here hoping to be . . . worthy of happiness."

"You asked to be beautiful?" wondered Olga, remembering the baron's dismissal of beauty and riches. It must have worked, because Anna was lovely. Her large eyes sparkled, and her flowing dark hair shone. Her long neck was graceful as a swan's. Her smiling lips and strong chin were captivating. "Were you granted what you wanted?"

"Yes. When I met Pavel, it was love that I found. Love that this valley granted me." With a swift movement Anna reached to take Olga's hands. "He is better and kinder than anyone I've ever met."

Pavel? Olga tried to understand what Anna was telling her, fitting the thoughts together like the pattern of a garment. She knew they were having fun at the ball—but love? Pavel was forgetful, and foolish, and smelly. That wasn't a tsarevich from one of Anna's stories.

In fairy tales the heroes were brave—which she supposed Pavel was—and loyal—he was that too—and honest. . . .

Oh dear.

Anna had come to the valley searching for love, and she had found it. Not the way she'd expected, but she'd found it all the same.

And for the first time Olga wondered if Pavel loved Anna too.

As if summoned, Pavel returned with refreshments. The song swelled to its conclusion, and the dancing couples clapped for the musicians. Amidst the applause, the baron's voice floated from the ballroom.

"My dearest guests," he began. Olga had the sensation of being wrapped in a warm blanket, of believing the baron truly treasured each and every one of his guests. How wonderful to feel special and cherished. Then she shook her head, remembering that this was all part of the baron's spell. He didn't care about his guests, and he didn't care about Olga. They were all pawns in his quest to lure his wife back, to re-create a life that didn't exist anymore.

As the baron spoke, Anna rose, trembling with excitement. Pavel extended his arm, and they made their way toward the ballroom, Olga trailing behind. She tried to catch Pavel's eye, but all his attention was directed toward the baron now. Was this the surprise he had spoken about?

The baron continued. "We have a musical treat for you tonight. First, I will sing a song familiar to many of you, and then we will have an extra performance from two very special guests."

There was a round of enthusiastic clapping as the baron gave a low bow.

The baron began his performance, filling the room with a rich baritone. He was right that the song was one people would know. Olga's heart twisted as she recognized a ballad her mother used to sing to her.

"When autumn winds blow,
The songbirds all know
To spread their wings wide,
So to escape the snow.

"But I shall hold strong, for
No matter how long
They are gone, there's a mark
On my heart of their song."

She wanted to step away from the room, to shut her ears. She had spent years trying not to remember her mother, feeling nothing but heartache at every memory. Pain at her loss, at the years of hunger and struggle that had followed, but also pain at Olga's own failures. After losing her mother, Olga had been broken and weak, needing to be rescued by Mr. Bulgakov. She didn't want to think of who she was then.

The baron's song finished, and Olga saw that many of her fellow guests were weeping at the mournful tale of loss and hardship. But Olga refused to let tears sting her own eyes.

"Now," said the baron, dabbing a handkerchief on his

cheeks, "please join me in welcoming Pavel and Anna to grace us with their gifts."

Applause rose to a swell, and Pavel and Anna approached the stage. Pavel turned to Olga with a meaningful glance, a joyful twinkle in his eye. One of the musicians handed Pavel his domra, and as they stepped onto the stage, he plucked it, the vibration of the strings ringing through the room.

Quickly, they began their song. Pavel played, and Anna sang at his side. Her voice had all the sweetness of a songbird's, and one glance at the other guests told Olga that people were delighted with the performance. Soon Pavel joined in singing, and his words and Anna's danced around each other, inter-twining, building in a crescendo.

> "... *Wherever you are, I am home.*
> *Together we're never alone.*"

The music swept through the crowd, ending at last to thunderous applause.

Olga raised her hands to clap but couldn't bring herself to make a sound. The song was the very one she and Pavel always sang together. The one he'd always had to pester her to sing.

Now it belonged to him and Anna.

Olga didn't speak to Pavel before leaving the ballroom. Something about the song had lit a fire in her. A seed of resentment had begun to sprout. Anna was taking Pavel away from her. And if Olga let it get much further, then Pavel might decide he wanted to stay here after all.

He was going to abandon Olga—she was sure of it. And she couldn't, wouldn't, let that happen.

She knew what she had to say to Mokosh. Olga wouldn't agree to help unless the spider queen could offer the Scarlet Heart in return. And she wanted an answer as soon as possible.

Instead of returning to her room, Olga filled her satchel with napkin-wrapped dumplings and marched through the gardens toward the forest. Pavel would have told her not to navigate the woods in the dark, that whatever she intended could wait until morning. But Mokosh's cave was less than an hour's walk away, and Olga had the glow of her magic to guide her.

The echoes of music from the distant ballroom drifted over the trees as she entered the shadows. "Can you lead me to your queen?" Olga asked, knowing that Pauk could hear her from her pocket.

The spider appeared and pointed a leg toward a dry creek bed. Olga plodded up it in silence, her breaths heavy as she climbed the slopes.

"Tell me," said the spider's soothing voice, and there was the tickle of tiny feet as Pauk crawled up her arm to sit on her shoulder, "what was it about the song they sang that upset you so?"

Olga huffed. "I don't want to talk about it."

"I sense you dislike Anna."

She didn't contradict him, instead pressing her lips tight together.

The spider was thoughtful a moment before finally saying, "I'm curious why you are dismissive of people believing in stories."

Her jaw ached from clenching as she considered her answer. "Stories aren't real. Wishes don't save people from starving." The words were bitter as Olga thought of how hard she'd had to fight, always, for everything she wanted, to avoid going hungry.

Branches clawed at them, and Olga swatted them away. The glow of her magic made the white birch bark shine, like spirits in a graveyard.

"Do you know," said Pauk softly, "why fairy tales always start with orphans? With people abused and neglected?"

Olga grunted.

"Answer the question."

Olga shook her head, ignoring the impulse to roll her eyes.

The spider cleared his throat. "Because the stories aren't about where they go, but about where they come from. What they leave behind, what they escape. The stories are about hope."

Those dark spider eyes seemed to see Olga's every fear, every wish, as he said, "Because even atop the highest tower, under the most dreadful curse, within the deepest part of the woods, there's always a way out."

fifteen

Olga parted the webs covering the cave entrance to find Mokosh asleep on her throne, her chin resting against her chest. She looked strangely vulnerable in this position despite the powerful magic she possessed. The fire had burned low, and Olga found a stick to stoke it. Mokosh woke at the crackle and pop of fresh wood catching alight.

"So soon. Does your return mean you intend to help?" Mokosh's question tapped cracks in Olga's reverie.

Olga didn't answer. She stared at the flames, feeling their warmth on her cheeks. It took her a moment to shake off her daze—she'd been thinking about Pavel and Anna, and what Anna's feelings meant for her and Pavel's plans. "That depends," she said finally. "I have no wish to learn about my family. But if, in exchange for my help, I ask for the jewel—the Scarlet Heart—could you offer it to me?"

Mokosh met Olga's gaze, steady and piercing. "You might find that what you want and what you need are one and the same," the spider queen said.

"Do you agree?" Olga said, keeping her voice firm. She wished Mr. Bulgakov could see how well accustomed she'd become to bargaining! He'd underestimated her for too long.

Anger flashed through the ancient woman's eyes. "This isn't a game, Olga. This is bigger than your treasure hunt."

The severity in Mokosh's voice was a flint igniting a roar of anger in Olga's stomach. "And what reason have you given me to trust you? The baron agreed to a bargain; you've only given me hints and lectures."

"You assume the worst of people because it's what you would do yourself. That says nothing about me." Mokosh had become calm, as hard as a stone in winter. "Magic is not about stealing from others. It's about what's inside your heart. And the strongest magic requires a full heart, something you seem in need of."

The words hit harder than a slap. Olga's hands clenched, and something pulsed in her temple. A full heart? What was *that* supposed to mean?

"Olga, maybe you should calm—" Pauk had scrambled from Olga's pocket and was tapping her shoulder with a spidery hand.

"No!" Olga shouted. She stomped toward the cave entrance. "We'll see how well you save your precious valley without my help then."

She didn't wait to hear if Mokosh called to her to stay. Her mind was a thundercloud as she stormed from the cave and back down the path to the palace. It took her a minute to realize that Pauk was still on her shoulder.

"Olga—" said Pauk. "Don't."

"Why are you still with me?" Olga snapped. "Don't you want to return to your queen? Do her bidding, since I won't?"

"I thought I could help you."

"Well, I don't want your help. I'd rather be on my own." The comments sounded harsher than she meant, but she refused to take them back. The spider queen's barbs had stung, and Olga didn't need a reminder.

The spider queen said Olga needed a "full heart." Which meant she'd put into words something that Olga had always feared about herself: She was incomplete. Broken.

"What are you going to do, Olga?" Pauk's voice was measured and steady.

Olga stared at him as though the answer were obvious. "Find the Scarlet Heart," she said.

The spider frowned at her, if one could call it a frown. "Is that all that really concerns you?" he asked. "After everything you now know?"

Olga couldn't help feeling a little ashamed. But soon her shame was masked with anger, its heat comforting and distracting.

"If we escaped, if we helped break the baron's spells, we'd be no better off than we were before," said Olga, gritting her teeth. "We'd be back with Mr. Bulgakov, traveling from town to town doing whatever we could to scrape by." She pulled at a stray thread on her satchel. "I don't want to go back to that. I want a different life—I want to make things better."

"There are other ways to make things better. Ways that have nothing to do with some jewel. You heard my queen—the valley is in peril!"

"I don't care about a valley, or the people in the palace, or a spider queen. I came here to find the jewel, and if you don't like it, then you can go away."

The effect of the words was immediate. The spider sank low on his thin legs. "I hope this story ends well for you."

"It will if I hold true to the plan."

Pauk had skittered down Olga's arm to the ground and hovered near the tip of Olga's boot. "Things aren't always so clean or clear. People are messy and tangled, just like their best-laid plans."

With that, the spider scampered through the grasses back in the direction of the cave.

Olga watched Pauk go, anger still pulsing through her veins.

She would get what she came here for. If only to prove them all wrong.

As Olga neared the base of the valley, something clattered nearby, and there was the low patter of voices and the snapping of twigs under boots. She ducked behind a log, lifting herself just enough to peer over its gnarled edge.

Three soldiers were walking, their weapons slung over their backs. Their faces were too shadowed for Olga to see. She sank again behind the fallen tree, keeping her breaths shallow, her ears tuned to the voices.

"I thought I saw something," said a soldier. They kept their voices low, and Olga had to strain to hear them over the pre-dawn chatter of the forest.

"You can't trust your eyes in this valley." This one sounded jittery and nervous.

"I don't trust *anything* here," said the third.

The first spoke again. "As well you shouldn't. We know people have disappeared. We can't allow that to happen to us too." There were footsteps, closer to Olga this time. They were searching the area. "Just keep your eyes peeled for anything un-usual so we can inform the magistrate. We're not to approach the palace until the others have arrived."

Olga held her breath, too afraid to move. Was this magis-trate the same one who had recognized Olga as a thief?

At last the soldiers continued on their path. Olga waited a long time before leaving her hiding place. Her mind was rac-ing to understand this new development. The soldiers were marching on the palace. How long would it take them to ar-rive? Days, hours? What did they have planned?

The sky had paled to the cool blue of predawn by the time Olga finally felt safe to move. Music drifted through the air and concluded with the usual applause.

When Olga approached the gate to the gardens, churning activity greeted her. The guests were leaving the ballroom for the night, but they weren't heading through the entrance hall toward the staircases and the upstairs guest wings. Instead, they were emerging from the palace into the garden, a steady flow of swishing dresses and sparkling necklaces.

Olga ducked behind the garden wall, not wanting to be seen.

The guests moved with the slow gait of revelers exhausted

from a long night of drink and dance, but there was something else fatiguing them. Some weight they all seemed to be carrying on their backs. They looked as though they were marching to their deaths.

And they were approaching *her*.

Quickly, Olga retreated to the edge of the forest, where she was still close enough to see the crowd but shadowed enough to escape their notice. Gone were the laughter and gaiety of the ballroom. They streamed through the gate in silence, footsteps heavy in the dewy grass.

Olga skimmed along the perimeter of the forest so that she could get a clearer view of their destination, stopping as a small crowd gathered by the lakeshore.

Glassy water reflected the bruised sky. It lit the faces of the people moving toward the water, illuminating their tired and wan expressions. As Olga watched, one by one they stepped out into the water, not bothering to remove their shoes or to lift their skirts. No one shivered or spoke. The twin boys didn't splash each other. The dozens of people simply clustered together, watching the mountains, waiting.

The sun emerged and light spilled onto the water. Orange tinged the surface, and like a stain spreading on silk, it reached their ankles, catching the ripples surrounding them. Silvery tendrils crept up their legs and chests, around their arms, their necks, clinging like ivy, binding them. The brightness forced Olga to shield her eyes for a moment. She blinked, trying to keep her eyelids open so she could watch what was happening.

Suspended in water and light, the people began to shift. Their necks grew longer, their arms broadened.

Olga wanted to look away, couldn't look away, had to look away. At last, when the brightness of the sunlight faded, she was able to see.

A bevy of swans glided across the rippling water.

And suddenly Olga knew the true nature of the curse affecting the people in this palace, the curse that had taken this entire valley. These people weren't simply sleeping the day away between balls.

They were spending their days as swans—as part of the baron's aviary collection.

OooEEEaaaooo.

The low cry emerged from the forest. Olga's memories darkened with visions of creatures with snarling mouths and red eyes. And the full truth dawned on her.

As the baron's hold on his magic crumbled, the swans too were turning into monsters, just like him.

sixteen

Olga crouched in silence, wondering what to do and where to go, trying to blend in with the edge of the trees, wishing she didn't suddenly feel so exposed. The sight of the swans' floating grace made her stomach churn. She now knew where the other guests disappeared to during the day. But that didn't align with what the baron had told her.

He had lied. It was all a lie.

Olga had asked the baron if people died when he used their heartstrings. He'd said no, but that wasn't the full truth.

A trembling spread through her and wouldn't stop. She found herself thinking of her mother's embrace, of warm arms wrapped around her whenever she was frightened.

But there was no one to comfort her. And so she wouldn't allow herself to be scared. She tamped the feeling down, even as the pain of it tore at her eyes and her throat.

Olga couldn't bring herself to return to the palace. Knowing the truth of what was happening and how Baron Sokolov's crumbling magic was affecting his guests, she struggled to move. Part of her wanted to race to Pavel's side, to demand that they leave the valley. But her mind still didn't trust her eyes. What if it was all a trick, another of the baron's illusions?

Instead, she remained by the lakeshore, watching the swans, searching for some sign of the truth in the beating of wings or the dip of a long neck. Above her, wrens chirped, flitting to and fro to snatch insects and to perch on branches. Their play was teasing, showing a freedom lost to the swans on the lake; a swan should be able to fly where it wishes, and yet they could not. Twigs jabbed at her where she sat. Dry grasses scratched her legs. Her stomach grumbled and she ate what food was in her satchel, ignoring the way it burned her throat when she swallowed.

Hours passed, and still Olga feared leaving the swans alone, worried that the baron would emerge to perform some new spell on them when they couldn't speak in protest. But exhaustion overtook her, and her eyes fluttered closed. When she awoke, the swans were gone.

She scrambled to her feet, fearful that harm had come to them. But a honk sounded in the distance, and as Olga crept toward it, she spotted a cluster of swans lurking inside the aviary. Most slept, seemingly oblivious to the storm raging in Olga's mind. She found a secluded place to keep watch, hidden behind a stout birch, and as midday shifted to afternoon and then early evening, her anxiety simmered. What if they didn't become human again? What if they were trapped this way forever, another piece of the baron's schemes?

Soon the sun hung low in the sky, a whole day gone. Olga watched, waiting. The palace to her right was silhouetted by the livid sky, silent as a skeleton without the music from the ball bringing it to life.

The swans waddled from the aviary toward the lake and clustered at the edge of the water, floating in the shallows amongst reeds swaying in the breeze.

When the sun kissed the horizon, the shadows of the mountains stretched across the lake. The fire of the sun's rays blazed on the swans' wings.

Screeches pierced the air.

And then they were morphing, their necks shrinking, their wings smoothing to skin. Olga's relief was short-lived when she saw the pain of the transformation. She forced herself to watch as their bodies contorted, as humans burst out of their feathery prisons. A wind howled through the valley. In the distance was the crash of a rockslide.

And then silence fell, like the moment between a nightmare's end and the reassurance of plump pillows and loving hands.

Humans stood ankle-deep in the lake, draped in glittering ball gowns. They picked weeds from their hair and smoothed their sleeves as they plodded along the marshy bank and onto dry land.

There was an instant, immediately after they transformed, when their faces betrayed their fear. Olga watched the person closest to her, the angular man with golden skin whom Olga recognized. The light deepened the lines of his frown. There was something akin to hopelessness in his eyes. It was a flicker that vanished swiftly, replaced by a blank and peaceful expression. The people stepped out of the water, now drawn toward the candlelight of the palace like moths.

They walked toward the garden gate and the ballroom beyond. The last in the line had a familiar sway to her gait, and Olga recognized Anna's dark tresses and round eyes.

Without stopping to think through what she was going to say, she rushed toward Anna and pulled her aside.

"Olga!" said Anna, her expression shifting from dreamy delight to one of stark surprise. "What are you doing here?"

"Do you remember?" said Olga.

"Remember what?"

"Do you know what the baron has done to you?"

With a quick glance over her shoulder, checking if anyone was listening, Anna pulled Olga farther from the others. Her fingers clasped Olga's arms.

"Don't, Olga," she said, a touch breathless. "It's not what you think."

"He's stealing from you. He's turned you into animals. And then he overwhelms you with magic and gives you food and music and dancing so that you forget everything!"

"I agreed to it, Olga—it's what I wanted!"

The chords of a minuet sailed toward them from the distant ballroom. The notes were light, but for Olga the ground trembled; the valley echoed.

Olga blinked. "You—you what?"

"Pavel wouldn't have given me a second look if I didn't

have what the baron granted me. He gave me beauty. Without it, I could never hope to have the kind of happiness people have in stories."

"Does Pavel know?"

Anna shook her head, the dark waves of her hair sweeping her shoulders. "Please—I don't want Pavel to learn the truth. He would try to end the curse, and I don't want to lose Pavel. My life is better here, thanks to Pavel and the baron. It's a price I'm willing to pay—"

Olga didn't want to hear any more. All the horror she'd felt at watching the people transform was overthrown by confusion.

"Olga, please," said Anna, reaching toward her. "Believe me, I don't want to lie or hurt Pavel. Haven't you ever wished that your life was different? That you could live your fantasy?"

Olga knew the feeling all too well, but she jerked her shoulder away. "You want lies. None of it's real, and you know it. Why should I believe anything you say?"

Anna didn't try to touch Olga again. She stepped back, opening and closing her mouth as if there was something she wished to say.

"Whatever it is," said Olga, "I don't want to hear it."

But Anna spoke anyway. "I might not remember this conversation when I go into the ballroom. That's part of the spell. Sadness seems to drift away along with the memory of what I am during the day. You can't blame me for wanting that."

There were footsteps and the clatter of the iron gate. Anna had gone. The music shifted, and Olga could hear the soft lilt of flutes on the wind.

She considered leaving—grabbing Pavel and walking through the woods and straight out of the valley. Or, if he chose Anna, leaving without him. She swallowed, trying to ignore the fear clawing at her insides. It was a losing battle.

But she had to hold fast to her plans. If she abandoned her mission of finding the Scarlet Heart, it felt like everything else would crumble around her. So she bit back her fears and retreated toward her rooms.

Her boots clunked against marble floors as she followed the secret paths she knew from her explorations. Hidden stairways helped her avoid the ballroom, and she climbed in a daze, still haunted by what she'd seen. Empty corridors and locked doors stood cold and forbidding as she followed them back to her room.

Olga entered to find the baron standing at her window, peering out over the lake's still waters. Moonlight shone over him, and Olga could clearly see the balance of truth and magic, the decaying human beneath layers of beautifully spun lies.

"I see you've discovered the truth of my friends here," the baron said, not turning to face Olga.

Olga tried to control her anger. Many years with Mr. Bulgakov had taught her that negotiations didn't work well when one was angry. She had to pretend to be confident. To remind the baron that she was someone worth dealing with.

She took a breath, steadying her nerves. One thing was certain: the baron was far more powerful—and dangerous—than Olga had given him credit for.

"Why?" she asked simply.

The baron turned. If he felt any surprise, he hid it well. "When they become swans, they forget who they are. It eases their worries, replenishes the power in their heartstrings more than ordinary rest ever could."

In that moment he reminded Olga of Mr. Bulgakov, teaching her that it didn't matter what she stole, or who she stole from. "And they are part of your collection."

A smile twitched on the baron's lips. "I told you they were the most unique species in my aviary. Swans were always my wife's favorites. She was the most beautiful creature I ever saw, and she loved anything as beautiful as she was. I wanted to create a place she would wish to return to, no matter the cost."

"The guests . . . they're the cost."

He clucked his tongue, looking at her like a disobedient

student. "The people here have what they want, and I get what I need in return: they replenish my magic and they grace my palace. You could have what you desire if you did what was necessary to take it."

Olga's anger threatened to reveal itself again, so she clenched her fists, standing firm. "We aren't the same," said Olga. "I wouldn't do what you do. Especially not once I learned what would happen to them in the end, that they become those . . . those creatures."

The baron's smile twisted, like he'd tasted something sour. "Would you not?" He moved across the room, his footsteps making no sound as they sank into the dense rug. As he approached Olga, he had to lean forward, almost doubling over, to bring his eyes level with her own.

"Everything that I have done," said the baron, "is for myself and my family. You are doing the same." Beneath the illusion of rosy skin and glittering eyes, his true form stirred. There was a low growl as the scales flexed and the hidden creature twitched, growing in size as if it wanted to expand and break through the illusion containing it.

He paused, as though he expected Olga to defend herself or disagree. When Olga stood silent, the baron clarified: "You seek to protect your friend, and you seek a jewel that will benefit yourself. You are doing nothing noble. And neither am I."

The words stung, but Olga understood the truth of them. Still, she wouldn't give the baron the satisfaction of agreeing.

He watched her, and for a moment his gaze softened. It was almost enough to make her believe some shred of humanity lingered in his corrupted heart. "I hope you never know the pain of losing what matters most to you. I'm trying to spare you that."

Olga was silent for a long moment. The thought of trusting him made her stomach lurch. "And I'm supposed to believe that you won't alter our bargain?"

"I offered you the jewel you seek, and I assured you that I would not use your friend's heartstring. I shall do as promised, if you do the same." He reached toward the door but stopped with a finger on the handle.

"Although," he said in a low, menacing snarl, "I can't vouch for *everyone* in the palace."

"What do you mean?"

"Your friend Pavel seems quite happy with his life here," the baron said delicately. "And he has found someone whose company he prefers to yours. Heartstrings are curious things. . . . If he falls in love, he might tie himself to her without meaning to."

With that parting remark, he was gone.

seventeen

The baron's words haunted Olga. She wanted to believe that he'd only meant to unnerve her.

But the risk was too great to ignore. There was no doubt that it was Anna the baron referred to. If Pavel was endangering himself by spending time with her, then their courtship had to end.

Pavel was social, a merrymaker. He enjoyed all kinds of people. But there was something different about how he behaved with Anna. His smile was brighter when he looked at her, his laughter unfettered. Unlike Olga, he didn't have a good eye for tricks and manipulations; that sort of skepticism wasn't in his nature. Olga saw now that he was in danger every moment he stayed in this palace, no matter what Baron Sokolov promised.

She wouldn't give up on her quest. But she couldn't let Pavel be trapped here either.

Late that night, when Pavel returned to his room, Olga was waiting for him. The candles had burned low, her eyes drooping as she dozed off. He stumbled into the room, his long legs dragging from a night of activity, his breath laced with wine. But he snapped to attention as he spotted Olga.

"I wondered where you'd disappeared to!" he said.

"You were distracted," said Olga, and she was surprised to hear a note of bitterness in her voice. She shook her head, trying to clear her words of emotion. "You seem to like Anna?" she asked.

Pavel plopped down on the bed beside her. "You want the truth?" he said.

"Always."

Delight pranced across his features, all traces of fatigue drifting away. He looked as if he were still dancing. "I think . . . I think I love her." He said the words slowly, as though he were unearthing buried treasure, brushing away the dust to reveal the truth of his own feelings. "She's the most wonderful person I've ever met. So funny, and clever, and kind, and she makes me feel like I can be those things too. Before coming here, I was always happy to drift along with Mr. Bulgakov's schemes. But when I met Anna, for the first time I felt that need—I wanted something for myself. I want to be with her."

Olga's suspicions were confirmed. He was besotted, and there was no good that could come of it, not appreciating the dangers of this place as Olga did. There was still time to protect Pavel from becoming trapped here, but that time was rapidly running out.

She took a breath, bracing herself to deliver the words he wouldn't want to hear. "You can't trust her," she said.

Pavel blinked. "What do you mean? Do you think she loves someone else? Do you worry she wouldn't be happy with me?"

He was too good, too kindhearted. Here he was, hearing Olga's warnings, and his first thought was to consider Anna's happiness.

"Not just her," said Olga. "You can't trust anyone here. This place is dangerous."

A long silence followed, and much as Olga wanted to say more, she allowed Pavel the space to ponder her words. Finally, he shook his head.

"I trust Anna," he said. "I'm telling you, I love her."

The memory flashed in Olga's mind of the swans transforming, with Anna emerging from the water. There were so many secrets Olga had kept from him about this place. Revealing the true danger of the palace meant admitting just how much she had kept hidden. She couldn't bear to see the disappointment fill his face on learning about her lies.

"You were supposed to stay focused on finding the treasure, and you couldn't even last a day," she said instead. "You're going to do something stupid to get yourself in trouble."

"Don't call me stupid," said Pavel.

"I'll say it if it's true," Olga snapped. "You're thinking with your heart, not your head."

She nearly fell over as the bed shifted under her. Pavel had stood suddenly, his fists trembling at his sides. "Someone has to!" he said. "You never care about anyone! Only yourself."

"That's not true," said Olga. "I care about you." Except . . .
Pavel did have a point. If forced to choose between herself and
Pavel, wouldn't she be a fool to choose Pavel? She'd always
thought there was nothing wrong with that; it was the only
way to survive. And besides, she was doing *this* for him. She
was protecting him.

One of Pavel's trembling hands rose to shield his eyes. "I'm
tired. Let's talk about this in the morning."

"You'll be asleep," said Olga. "We need to talk about
it now."

"Olga, leave."

She stared at him, and stood to face him, planting her feet
squarely.

"*Leave,*" he said. And though Pavel would never threaten
her, or shout, or hit, the word knocked the air from her lungs.
They'd been inseparable most of their lives. And now he was
choosing Anna over her. He was refusing to listen, even as she
fought to protect him.

Without another word, Olga stomped from the room, slam-
ming the door behind her.

Back in her own chamber, Olga paced back and forth, like
an animal trapped in a cage. There had to be some way to convince Pavel that he needed to leave the palace. He could return
to Mr. Bulgakov, or wait for Olga somewhere until she had
obtained the jewel. But he would never agree to leave Anna
behind. He was too trusting. Too loving.

Unless she could convince him that Anna didn't want
his love.

A terrible thought struck Olga, and at first she tried to

brush it away. But the longer she stood in her large and lonely room, the more it felt like the safest way to protect him.

Pavel was falling in love with Anna—that much was obvious. But if Anna was the one to push him away, he'd have to believe her.

Olga remembered Pauk's lesson, how she could combine magic with real things to create a spell that was stronger than one she could achieve with her heartstring alone. An idea had begun to form, of a spell that just might save Pavel from himself.

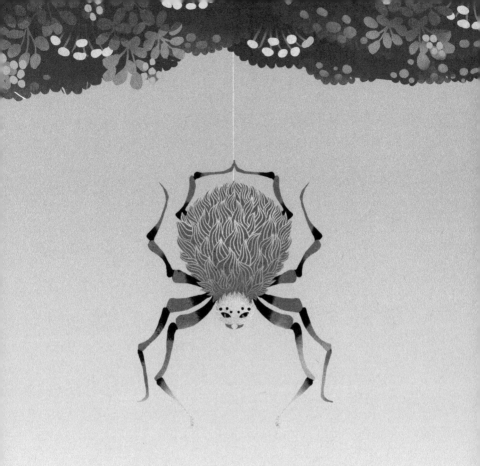

The Spider Spins
His Sixth Tale

I wish to remind you, little ones, of the swan I spoke of before. This swan had begun to notice a change in her peaceful
life on the lake. It all started the day she was rescued by the
humans, when pain interrupted the dreamy cycle of dawn till
dusk, when there was little to concern her but what meal she
would have next.

The swans around her were changing. The swan wished
she could understand, wished she could prevent this, but
change is a powerful force, an inevitable one, an unstoppable
one. Change comes in the form of a hunter's arrow, or a flood of
water, or a careless wish. It comes when a new person enters
our life and breaks open the protective spell we wrap around
ourselves.

The swan watched her companions, how they dragged
themselves through the water as if it were mud. But one among
their number was sicklier than the rest—he could barely swim
an inch from the bank. The swan approached him, nudging
him with her bill, encouraging him to eat. She snatched weeds
from the shore and extended her long neck to offer them.

But the sickly swan didn't seem to see them. His eyes were
glassy, his movements confused. Like he was losing himself.

Something about this place was wearing him down, like
water rubbing away at a riverbank.

The swan could no longer ignore the fear tumbling inside
her. But she didn't know what to do, or where to turn. She

was starting to feel trapped, with threats all around her. And worse, she felt her own thoughts slipping. Like she was becoming less herself, thoughts blurring into indistinct shapes, like shadows beneath the murky water.

The swan knew she needed to do something, but she was battling against an enemy she couldn't see. She didn't know how to break free, but she could fight to hold on.

I am not asking a question, little ones, I am telling you now: There is a bravery to holding on, even when one can't see the light. Even when one doesn't know how the curse can be broken, or when. The swan fought to remember, fought for herself. And that is braver than any bogatyr.

eighteen

Specks of dust and magic glinted in the afternoon air as Olga retraced her steps to the room she sought in the servants' wing. Sleep had eluded her, and now only a few hours remained for Olga to enact her plan.

On their first day exploring the palace, Olga and Pavel had discovered a sewing room. Now, after a few wrong turns, she managed to find it again. Though some of the fabrics had clearly deteriorated over the years, there were still remnants of what had once been a seamstress's paradise.

There were enormous bolts of muslin, wool, and velvet, some of it now moth-eaten, but many of the bolts still beautifully intact. A large rack displayed threads of every color imaginable in varying weights. Embroidery floss. Fine sewing threads. Yarns for cross-stitching.

She grabbed several spools and shoved them into her satchel, then took a bolt with enough fabric to suit her needs, carrying it through the hallways back to her room.

As a bell counted down the hours until the ball, Olga

grabbed a needle and thread and set to work. The excitement of trying this magic pulsed through her. The magic thrummed, a heartbeat flowing through her heartstring.

It was nearly nightfall by the time Olga finished. Her neck and hands ached from hunching over for more than five hours. And despite using only a fraction of her magic, it had still been enough to exhaust her.

She shook out the cloak, letting it tumble to the floor before her. The pale fabric seemed to absorb all the light around it, making the room appear darker in its presence. The stitching was perfect, every inch even and flowing. It was the finest work Olga had ever done, and she was using it for a purpose more sinister than she had ever imagined.

With a swift motion, she stood and swept it over her shoulders.

A mirror stood in the corner of this room. Looking at her reflection was never something she enjoyed very much. But this time she approached without hesitation, just anxious excitement. She had no idea if the magic was going to work, and she wasn't sure if she wanted it to.

But as she stepped in front of the mirror, it was the image of Anna staring back at her. Olga moved her cloak, and the Anna in the mirror moved hers. The hands in the mirror had slender fingers that moved as Olga's hands moved. And the face that stared back at her was Anna's, wide-eyed with shock instead of her usual joyful enthusiasm. Long hair fell to her waist in flowing waves. She was beautiful.

The spell had worked. Combining her magic with her sewing meant that Olga could create spells far more complex than

anything she had ever attempted before. It was a magic that was uniquely hers, and it terrified her.

Yet the thought of what she had to do next frightened her even more.

Cool air brushed Olga's cheeks, and she tugged the cloak around her shoulders.

The sun had set, and the ballroom was alive with music and laughter. But Olga was outside in the garden, knowing that this was where Pavel and Anna met every night as the festivities began.

Carefully, Olga crept down the pebbled pathway, footsteps

crunching as she went. The shadows were dense between the hulking hedges on either side of her.

She passed a row of topiaries, and a sculpted horse glared at her with empty leafy eyes. Hurrying past, Olga clutched the cloak tighter and approached the fountain where she would wait for Pavel.

Olga looked down at her hands. They were her own. But reflected in the water, they were larger, with long, slender fingers. The image was an illusion, like the one she'd performed on the music box she'd sold to the little boy and girl. That felt so long ago, even though it had been no more than a week.

There was a rustle in the hedges behind her, and the snap of a twig. Pavel emerged from an unseen path, wearing traveling boots and a large pack strapped to his shoulders. There was a look of irrepressible excitement and love in his eyes, in the curve of his smile.

"Anna," he said, stepping forward to take her hands. "I'm going to say this now, before I lose my nerve." He took a deep breath. "I want you to run away with me."

Her heart pinched. Pavel was going to leave without even saying goodbye. Deep inside her, a monster growled, seething with jealousy. Pavel was like a brother to her, and he was going to run away. He was finally going to leave Olga behind—for Anna. The monster growled again, louder this time.

Olga frowned and tore her gaze from his. "Don't," she said. It was difficult to say much when the words were trapped in her throat.

She forced herself to think of the goal behind all this: the Scarlet Heart. Pavel had long since forgotten their purpose, and he was endangering himself. Olga was doing him a favor by protecting him. Her stomach churned with anger. And, she realized, with hurt.

"What's wrong?" he asked, a crease forming between his brows.

The longer she stood there and the more she talked, the more risk of Pavel sensing something amiss. "I can't go with you," she said. She knew the words didn't sound like Anna's. She couldn't speak with Anna's excitement, her musicality. She closed her lips tight again.

Pavel's expression was thoughtful and tender. "I know it's frightening. I can't give you much, but I can give you my love." He tilted his head, trying to stare into Olga's eyes, but she turned away. If she saw the love in his gaze, it might make her doubt her purpose.

The thought further fueled her anger. Pavel had allowed himself to get distracted. He was a fool to let himself fall in love. He refused to see what was so obviously untrustworthy about this palace, this valley, these people.

A nagging voice reminded Olga that if she had trusted him with the truth, then perhaps things wouldn't have gotten this far. But she brushed the voice away.

"It won't work that way," she said.

Surprise shot from him like a spark. Pavel took his hands away from hers and began to pace. "What's gotten into you? This doesn't sound like you at all," he said.

Olga's heart began thumping so loudly, she was sure he could hear it. What would happen if Pavel saw through the magic disguising her? She needed to end this quickly. She tried to remember everything Mr. Bulgakov had taught her, every-thing about convincing without revealing the truth, about being charming, and lovable, and believable. All the ways she'd learned to manipulate people to swindle them. All the illusions. "The truth is: I don't love you."

Pavel stared at her, his green eyes a thunderstorm of hurt. This was the part that Olga really didn't want to say. But she knew that it would get Pavel to go away, and she was running out of time—he wasn't leaving. She swallowed, bracing herself to say the wicked words. "You're just not the prince that I imagined I'd fall in love with."

Pavel winced as if she'd slapped him. He turned, his face collapsing, crushed. He couldn't even look at her. Then he grabbed his bag, his shoulders heaving, and stumbled down the path the way he'd come without another word.

Olga stamped the ground and clawed her fingers through her hair. This was who Mr. Bulgakov had taught her to be—someone ruthless, heartless. And the baron had shown her the same. Keeping her focus on what she wanted meant difficult choices, harsh words. But part of her wanted to sob, to scream, to race after Pavel and tell him that no, this was all a lie. It was what Pavel would have done. He would have told the truth.

But that was what made him weak. And much as it hurt her heart to hurt him, she knew that he had to leave the valley. It was the only way to keep him safe.

She hadn't realized how much time had passed until a soft voice called out from nearby.

"Pavel," someone whispered. "Pavel, are you there?"

Panic blinded Olga as she recognized that voice. The last thing she needed was for Anna to come and find the image of herself staring back at her.

Olga pulled at the cloak, but her shaking hands couldn't clasp the fabric, and it caught on her hair. Finally, she yanked the cloak over her head and managed to duck behind a hedge just in time. Anna appeared in a shimmering party dress that flared out like the petals of a peony, looking every bit the story-book princess.

Heeled shoes clacked against the paving stones like the tick of a clock as Anna paced. She sighed, then sat on the edge of the fountain in a swell of skirts, only to rise a second later to resume her pacing. Music rang out from inside the palace, yet Anna waited.

Olga watched in silence, refusing to tell Anna that Pavel was gone, and that she had told him to go.

Olga stuffed the cloak into her bag as she stepped into the candlelit glow of the ballroom. Her chest was tight, and it only clenched tighter at the loud music scratching against her ears.

She couldn't bring herself to think of the hurt on Pavel's face, or of Anna's disappointment. What she had done would keep Pavel safe. She couldn't regret that, even if it meant hurting him.

Could she?

He had intended to leave her behind. He was going to run away with Anna. And Olga could have let him, but she hadn't. Instead, she'd broken his and Anna's hearts.

Something like remorse stung the back of Olga's throat. She swallowed, ignoring it. Pavel was safe—that was what mattered.

The others in the ballroom seemed to be enjoying themselves as though nothing had changed: feasting in the banquet hall, swirling through the ballroom. But the room felt emptier without Pavel and Anna at its center. Their laughter and happiness had drawn people in like a campfire on a winter's night, and the room was darker without them.

It was only now that Olga saw how the expressions on the faces of the other guests seemed to lack joy, anger, heartache, sorrow. They were filled with nothing, because the baron had taken everything from them.

She didn't want to wait for Anna to enter the ballroom, couldn't face the thought of meeting her and trying to avoid her questions about Pavel. Instead, Olga found herself retracing the familiar steps to the aviary. She hadn't been there since her bargain with the baron, before she'd learned the truth of his swans.

Olga had first encountered the mysteries of this palace in the aviary. It was where the swans gathered during the day. It was mere steps from where the baron had crafted his spells. It felt like the aviary was the center of the baron's web, and it still held secrets she had yet to uncover.

But as she stepped into the grand room covered by its gilded cage, Olga found that the baron was already here. And he wasn't alone.

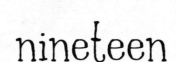

nineteen

O lga emerged from the corridor to find the baron on his hands and knees on the stone floor of the aviary. Before him was a swan, threads of magic unspooling from its neck and wings, revealing flashes of a monster's red eyes and scaled wings.

The baron's arms trembled; his breaths were labored and wheezing. He clenched a strand of magic attached to the creature, trying to keep hold of it. But it was slipping from his grasp.

The creature was gaining control. And something had gone terribly wrong, because it should have returned to its human form by now.

She rushed forward, reaching toward the strand. "You're losing control. Let me—"

But the baron glowered at her, and there was something in his eyes that chilled her. It looked remarkably like fear.

He pushed her away wildly. "No, Olga! Get out of here!"

She stumbled back, nearly falling on the stone and scraping

her hands, but she refused to leave. "We have to make it human again!"

Before he could answer, the creature screeched, pulling away from the baron, yanking the magic out of his hold. The baron fell forward, and as if an earthquake had roiled through his bones and muscles, he twitched, biting back screams of pain.

Fumbling, he managed to grab hold of the magic once more, and the tremors stopped. He stilled but for the panting, trembling like a wounded animal. His hands shifted to regain their control over the strand as the creature began to thrash against its captivity again.

"It's too late," he spat. With labored movements, he began to yank at the strand of magic coming from the creature. As he did, the magic further unraveled.

"Wh-what are you doing?" For the first time in her memory, Olga found herself at a loss for words.

"If I keep the connection, the corruption will poison me and then the whole flock. We'll all become creatures like this one. Severing the magic buys us all more time."

And if he did . . . She knew without asking, as sure as she knew her own heartstring, that the person would be trapped as a creature forever.

"So once you use up their magic, you trap them like this? They won't become human anymore."

There was no time for thought. Olga ran forward and pushed the baron away, causing him to lose his hold on the strand. "You won't!" she shouted at him, anger pulsing through her. "That's a person, someone you've trapped in this form!"

"I'll lose hold if I don't." The words tore from his throat. "Once the magic starts to decay, I have to cut them away. They could destroy the whole palace." He threw himself back at the string and began pulling once more.

The creature snarled, thrashing against the heaving of the magic. Then it lurched, snapping its jaws at Olga. She leapt backward, remembering the fear that had shot through her when she was chased by those monsters in the forest. Its red eyes glared at her, and she felt a sting of heartbreak at the realization that those had once been human eyes. Inside this creature there was a person, someone who was probably as terrified as she was.

"How many have you cut away? How many of them haunt the forest?"

He didn't answer, and he didn't need to, for she knew that any number was unforgivable. With a final yank, he severed the thread between himself and the creature. It collapsed against the stones of the aviary floor. With heartless cruelty, the baron opened the gate leading out to the forest and used his magic to thrust the unconscious animal outside.

She'd failed to stop him.

"This was never our bargain," she said, finding some sort of strength inside her that burned with a hot fury. "I agreed to help you bring people here, not to help you turn them into these creatures."

The baron scoffed. "We only discussed what you would do and what it would earn you in return. This has nothing to do with our bargain."

"You need me," said Olga. "I could stop right now, and you'd lose everything."

"Then go," he said.

"I won't until I have what I was promised. I want the Scarlet Heart."

The baron barked a laugh. "Always the shrewd negotiator!" His eyes were piercing in the darkness, and he watched her in silence for a moment, deciding something. Then a smirk crept into those bottomless eyes, and once again Olga thought she could glimpse gray scales between the frayed spots in his magic. "You poor little fool. I don't suppose it matters now," he said. "Come with me."

Something in his calm demeanor chilled her. It was as if the treasure didn't mean anything at all to him. She tensed, wondering if this was some sort of trick. There had to be a catch if he was giving in so easily.

With quick footsteps, he led Olga along the corridor. She recognized that he was leading her to the same secret room where they had first made their bargain. She wished that she had been able to search the room herself. He had been keeping the Scarlet Heart here all this time? It was so obvious.

He led her inside the room, where the water in the bowl cast its ghostly green glow.

"Now close your eyes," said the baron.

"No," said Olga. "I want to know that you're not holding anything back. That you aren't planning to use illusions to trick me so you can fail to honor our agreement."

At this, Baron Sokolov laughed again, his voice echoing

around the dank chamber. "Of course," he said. "Then let me show you."

He took her toward the desk covered in papers. His fingers slid along its back until they found a hidden catch and a compartment in the wood opened. Out slid a lidless box lined with velvet. At first, Olga thought it was empty. But when she looked closer, she saw it contained a single necklace, a gold locket on a fine chain.

"My treasure," he said, holding it up to her. The locket danced in the air, glinting in the pale light.

Olga searched for signs of a jewel but saw nothing. "Is it gold?" she asked.

"Yes, but that is not its value," he said. A smile disguised the sneer at his lips. "You were driven to come here because you had heard stories of the Scarlet Heart, yes? A gem that the tsar himself envied. That jewel," he said, "was my wife. My wife, who was said to be the jewel of this valley. This necklace is nothing more than a token of my love for her. Her portrait is inside."

The locket spun on the end of the chain, teasing Olga. It was shut tight, and she couldn't see the portrait. She wasn't sure she would ever want to. The baron was right: she'd been a fool.

"It is my wife that you sought, nothing more. But you may take this." He offered it to her as if it meant nothing. "I no longer have need of it, or your assistance. There are soldiers entering this valley as we speak, and when they come, I will have enough people to feed my magic and extend it across the entire tsardom. Soon I will bring home my wife and child in the flesh."

Olga took the dangling locket from him, her heart sinking. All this time, and she had been searching for something that didn't exist. Not truly. She had a locket that meant nothing to her, of a woman she would never meet. "Your wife and child were never anything more than ornaments to you," she said. "Just like those people are only birds in your collection. We're just treasures for you to possess."

With silent steps, Olga retreated.

The baron called out to her as she reached the door, *"They* were treasures. *You* are nothing." His voice echoed against his laboratory's stone walls.

She did not answer as she let the door close behind her.

She had to leave. There was nothing keeping her here now, and if she hurried, she might be able to catch up with Pavel. But something weighed on her, as though she were tethered by the baron's magic. She was being pulled in two directions, and she felt completely lost.

Olga slipped out into the aviary. The night air bit her lungs. She opened the gate leading to the forest, the cold iron hard against her palm.

Something moved just beyond the gate. Figures in a tight formation, glowing white as moonlight. She crept forward and saw a cluster of the creatures watching her from the edge of the forest.

Her heart drummed a heavy rhythm. They held still, watching her with blood-red eyes.

Their leader came closer. It didn't look ready to attack, but she could see the slits of its pupils as it approached, its sharp talons and pointed teeth. And something else. Its features were distorted with fury, monstrous, but buried deep within it was a human still. Was it possible it could become human again?

She reached forward with a trembling hand, trying to show the creature that she meant no harm. The creature would not allow her to touch its scaly feathers, nor did it retreat. It merely hovered, watching her. She wished she could hear its thoughts, then imagined that if she could, she would hear a plea for help.

But she didn't know how.

As if sensing her resignation, the leader moved away from her, and soon the others followed, disappearing into the forest.

Dazedly, she made her way back to the ballroom. The festivities were well underway as she neared. Music danced on the air; hollow laughter tinkled like bells. She was sure that, like everything else in this place, the guests' joy was empty as a leaky barrel. The trades he gave these people paled in comparison to what he had taken from them.

But underneath the clang of instruments, something boomed in the entrance hall. There was the rattling clank of footsteps.

Every head in the room turned.

At the three double doors leading into the entrance hall, a crowd was gathering. Soldiers, each fully armored in the

raiment of the regional guard, stood at attention. At their head was a face Olga recognized: Magistrate Morozova, who'd accused her of stealing at the market what felt like ages ago.

And standing beside her was Mr. Bulgakov.

Olga fought to swallow the feelings that bubbled up inside her at the sight of him. What had her former guardian done? Had he reported her to the magistrate for some kind of personal gain?

As quickly as she could, she slipped between members of the crowd, creeping toward one of the large doors leading out to the garden.

She needed to get away, as fast as possible. But she burned to know what was going to happen, why the soldiers were here. Once she'd entered the darkness of the garden, she stopped, ducking behind one of the enormous hedges. If she squinted, she could just peek through the leaves to see inside.

Soldiers marched into the room, all clanging metal and barked orders. The dancers faltered and laughter slowed to a halt as everyone heeded the newcomers' approach.

The magistrate waited until complete silence had fallen before she spoke. Even the echoes from the musical instruments were dampened. "There are rumors of a curse in this valley," she announced. She waited, as if to unearth the evil magic based on the reactions of the onlookers. "No one is to come or go until we understand what is going on here."

"My dear guests," said Baron Sokolov. He had emerged from the crowd, approaching the magistrate. He still looked less polished than usual after his ordeal in the aviary, with several of his white hairs out of place, but for the magistrate he was all jolly smiles and ease. The two of them were nearly the same height—the magistrate watched his approach with skepticism stitched into the curl of her lips, the clench of her jaw.

But the baron had taken on the persona of the charming old man Olga had met when she'd first come to the palace. Was the kindness always a front, or had it been his true demeanor before losing his wife and child?

"What an honor that you've decided to join us. I hope you agree there's no cause for concern in this valley or in my palace. We are simply enjoying a night of feasting and dancing." He motioned to the guests surrounding him and continued his practiced speech. "It is my deepest sorrow to confirm that our festivities are about to conclude. But you are most welcome to join us when the ball continues tomorrow night." He patted his pockets. "Oh, dear me, I seem to have misplaced my watch. I could use your assistance in ensuring the ball begins on time!"

The magistrate's face softened at his welcome, a clue that she too was getting swept away in the magic. Then something shifted, and she shook her head for a moment as if she'd glimpsed the illusion. "I will need to ask you some questions," she said, her voice more confident. "Are you Baron Sokolov? Our records show you as the last of your family to reside here."

"Indeed!" The baron withdrew his handkerchief to dab his glistening forehead. He fluffed it with a flourish before returning it to his pocket. "And of course I will do everything in my power to help you in your search. You are most welcome to stay here in my palace, to slumber in my rooms, to savor my feasts. Your esteemed efforts demand a reward, and you must join us as our honored guests tomorrow evening."

All traces of suspicion seemed to drain away from the magistrate, and Olga knew that the woman was lost. His words were working, his illusions swaddling her. The soldiers too were looking around them as if they would love nothing more than to join in the ball at once.

"Thank you, your lordship," she said, "for your hospitality. Yes, we will gladly be led to your guest rooms. And then I can discuss with you how to proceed with our search of the valley."

"Wonderful!" said Baron Sokolov. "I will have my servants guide you." He clapped his hands, and figures who had moments ago been carrying around food on trays appeared near the doors to the ballroom to lead the soldiers away. Mr. Bulgakov too joined them, and Olga's nerves pinched in wonder at his motives. The baron stood silently, unmoving, as they retreated from the room.

Olga needed to do something, to warn someone. The soldiers were walking straight into the baron's trap.

She had to find a way to get to the soldiers without the baron seeing. She needed to tell them that the baron was not to be trusted. She wished Pavel were here to guide her—he always knew which path to take, where to place his footsteps so that others didn't notice them. But as she stepped back, the tip of Olga's boot caught on an uneven stone and she fell, her hands slapping the ground.

There was the crunch of gravel underfoot, and she turned to see the baron watching her.

"It's a pity for you that you didn't escape when you had the chance," he said.

twenty

The baron's eyes reflected the deep blue of the lightening sky.

Olga knew what he was going to do before he did it, and she snapped a hand toward her heart, ready to snatch a length of magic. But he was too quick. She barely saw his hand touch his chest before his magic struck as powerful as lightning, slashing through the air to tighten around her. The magic crackled as it bound her wrists.

She wanted to shout for help, but there was no one she could turn to. The guests had abandoned the ballroom. The soldiers had retired to the guest rooms upstairs.

"They're looking for the source of the curse. They'll figure out that it's you," Olga said as she wrestled against the strands ensnaring her.

"Tell me," he said with a smirk, "if you told them my plans, who do you think they'd believe? Me—a baron; or you—the wanted thief?"

He had planned this. He'd told her in his laboratory that

he knew the soldiers were coming. "You're going to take them all . . . ," she said.

His smile did not reach his eyes, and the evil that lurked inside him stirred. "Of course," said the baron. "How fortunate that your old guardian met Magistrate Morozova on the road and led such a large group of people straight to me. It would have taken years for me to accrue so many heartstrings, but now I shall gather them all at once."

"Your magic can't contain the strings you hold already," said Olga. "How do you expect to take these soldiers without losing your grip?"

"What you saw earlier in my aviary," he said, each word dangerous, "was my solution. I shall cut loose those who have lost their value, and with so many new guests entering the valley, I can feed their heartstrings to my spell like kindling to a flame."

And if he did, everyone would get burned.

"And what do you intend to do with me?" she asked. Fear was cascading through her with all the force of a rockslide. It hurt to breathe, to blink.

"Oh, I haven't decided. Those creatures in the forest might be hungry. Or there's always the lake."

As she stood before the baron, an expendable pawn in his plans, Olga realized she should have seen this coming all along. She'd thought herself so clever and conniving, but she'd underestimated what lengths the baron was willing to go to. Playing deadly games yielded only deadly rewards.

No matter how she wiggled or twisted, the baron's magic

held firm. Slowly, he guided her through the palace and down toward the cellars.

A door clanged open and Olga found herself released from her bonds and shoved down a set of stairs. She stumbled but managed not to fall. It was her last chance at dignity, and she turned to give the baron a look of hatred before he closed the door and locked it.

Darkness descended as she was sealed inside. The baron hadn't taken her satchel, but there was nothing inside it that could help her now. Her trembling fingers pulled a humming strand from her chest to use as a torch, and in its glow Olga recognized the crypt that she had explored with Pavel. Unease filled her as she beheld the engravings on the walls. Faceless names, generations long forgotten. Just like she would be.

The hatred she'd briefly donned as a mask drifted away. She was tired, too tired to feel anything but anger at herself.

A sickness seeped inside her stomach. She'd done to Pavel what the baron did to everyone. She'd told herself that a bargain with the baron would help them both. But deep down it had always been to get what she wanted. And then she'd tricked Pavel and destroyed his happiness with Anna.

In her travels with Mr. Bulgakov, Olga had tried to distance herself from the people they were swindling. She'd thought of them as tools to help or hinder her. But this was Pavel, her best—and only—friend. When had she started treating him like little more than a tool she could use in crafting her own plans?

A desire greater than anything she'd felt before clamped

hold of her: the wish to tell Pavel that she wanted his friend-ship not because of what he could do for her, but because she cared about him.

There was nowhere to sit or sleep but the floor, nothing but a small hole high in the wall to let in fresh air. She sank to the hard ground and buried her face against her knees.

Everything—and everyone—that truly mattered was gone.

Hours had passed in the cold cell before Olga remembered the locket the baron had given her, and she pulled it out to inspect it. The metal was cold in her hands, light as air. She held it close to her nose in the dim light.

It was gold, at least. That was something. She could pawn it to book passage on a ship, perhaps. Or she could purchase a loom and sell fabrics. But that required escaping from this place.

She ran her fingers along the image engraved on the locket's front, a bird in flight, remembering how the baron had said that his wife had loved birds. She hoped his wife and child were living happily wherever they had gone; but more important, she hoped they would not be lured back against their will.

Olga knew how it felt to be in a life that she didn't want to lead, to yearn to escape. And she wanted that escape for them.

The tips of her fingers pinched the clasp and she twisted, opening the locket.

Her heart nearly stopped.

A heartstring uncoiled from within. But that wasn't what had stolen her breath away.

Inside was a portrait drawn in simple ink and watercolor. And the resemblance was unmistakable. The nose, the cheeks. She recognized the twinkling eyes, the half smile. The curls of auburn hair artfully arranged around the neck and shoulders.

The face in the locket belonged to her mother.

Questions and answers flooded Olga's mind.

The baron had spoken of his wife running away with their unborn child. He wanted them because they belonged to him, and he needed them. His jewel. His heir.

If the wife was Olga's mother, then the child had to be her. His daughter. The baron was her father. And he'd never abandoned her—in fact, he'd spent years searching for her, but it was her mother who did not want to be found. And Olga had been in this palace for days—spoken to him, bargained with him—neither of them knowing how they were connected.

With a strange whooshing feeling, she realized that this was her home.

She was wanted. But the person who wanted her was a monster.

This was what Mokosh had meant. The spider queen had tried to tell her, had hinted that Olga was close to discovering the truth about her family.

And the baron—her father—in his desperation to reunite their family had done unspeakable things, trapped all these people and unleashed a blight upon the valley. All to find her.

The guilt of it pressed in on her. Crushed her.

Pavel was gone. He wasn't here to tell her to do the right thing, because Olga had sent him away. But now, without him by her side, she wanted to do what would make him proud, even if he never had a chance to know it.

But it was too late.

The problem she faced was as solid and impenetrable as the walls around her. Olga sat silently in the little room as her heartbeats counted the passing seconds.

Lost and frightened, she sank into an uneasy sleep.

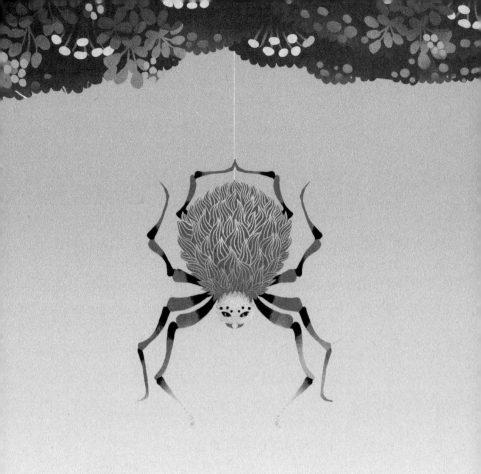

The Spider Spins
His Seventh Tale

It is late, little ones, and I am afraid we are coming close to the end of our story time. But there is another tale I wish you would know, of a woman who loved her daughter very much. From the first moments of feeling the child in her belly, she was overcome by a love that could move mountains and break curses. A love stronger even than the magic thread in her heart.

Before this, her life had been a dream filled with lavish parties, luxuries, and a husband who was unafraid to declare his adoration of her before the world. But there had always been a worry at the back of her mind: that his love was only for her beauty and her magic.

And now, her understanding of love had changed. She felt a need to protect her child above all else, and when she heard her husband speak of the future—of his plans to seize the throne and name their child as tsar, and how those plans treated their child like a pawn in a chess game—she began to wonder if her husband knew what it was to love.

As the birth day grew nearer, so her own protectiveness grew. And so did her husband's ambitions. Until one day, she realized that she could not protect her child and remain where she was. So she left, and she did what she could to ensure that he would not follow.

Knowing what happened next as you do, I ask you, little ones, did she make the right choice?

twenty-one

*O*lga was glued inside a sticky cocoon of magic. Threads
surrounded her, and no matter which way she moved, they
tied her in place. She pulled and yanked, but still they
held fast. The shimmering strands spread in an elaborate web.

"Olga!" shouted a familiar voice.

And suddenly she teetered at the edge of a cliff above an inky
darkness. Pavel stood ahead of her, his feet planted on the solid
ground, while the earth beneath Olga was crumbling.

All the threads had disappeared save for one. A single thread
connected Olga and Pavel, and it shone with a steady glow.

As the earth fell away beneath her, Olga felt the thread tying
her to Pavel pull taut. Pavel shouted, his voice sharp with fright,
and he extended his hand. His fingers nearly brushed hers.

The last of the cliffside tumbled away, and Olga was falling.

The thread connecting her and Pavel snapped.

Down, down, down she fell, the darkness consuming her
screams.

A sudden hissing sound woke her. Was it a snake? A rat? Some sort of hissing spider? She waved her magical torch around her, searching the shadows.

Then the hissing sounded again. It was coming from the hole high in the wall of the crypt.

"*Psst!* Olga, are you there?" said a voice. Her heart jumped as she recognized Pavel.

She sat up, looking toward the tiny opening. It couldn't be more than the size of her fist, enough to let fresh air into the room and nothing more. Still, the sound lifted her spirits like warm stew on a frigid night.

"Is it really you?" she asked, trying to keep her voice to a whisper.

"Olga! Can you hear me?" Pavel was losing the battle at keeping his voice low. He was a big person, and he had a big voice.

Olga winced. "Yes. But you have to get away from here," she said. "If I can hear you, someone else will hear you too."

"They're all still asleep. The ball only ended a few hours ago," he said. "It'll be okay, Olga—we just have to get you out of here."

Olga's tears intensified. She hiccuped. She hadn't thought that he would come. She hadn't thought that anyone would come.

And now here he was.

But he was in danger because of her. He needed to get away from here.

"If you try to get me out, they'll find you and then we'll all be in danger."

"I'm not going to leave you behind," said Pavel.

And she knew that he wouldn't, and he never would. He had proven it to her over and over, with his actions and his words.

"I'm not sure there's a way out of here," said Olga. "He's locked me in."

"I've brought a friend who can help," said Pavel, and there was a touch of nervous laughter, and disgust, in his voice. "Meet me at the top of the stairs."

Olga heard the skittering of many small legs against stone walls, and then Pauk appeared at the opening, a key tied with spider silk to his hairy back. Olga's heart leapt at the sight of him. She had assumed the spider would be angry at her too.

Pauk descended on a glittering thread from the hole and down to Olga's feet. Olga could have kissed him. Where did one kiss a spider? She was glad that Pavel wasn't inside the cell and able to see what joy did to her. He'd never let her live it down.

Together they approached the door. But the baron had anticipated her—of course he had. The lock was bound in magic, just like the door to his secret room. Strands of magic were tangled around the handle, pulsing with such intensity that Olga was afraid they would burn her if she touched them.

"Not to worry," said Pauk, and Olga's alarm subsided. The

spider began to weave his own magic, draping glimmering threads around the lock and handle. He looped around, deftly ducking between the baron's strands without touching them, knitting a pattern more ornate than any embroidery. Starbursts, crosses, crescents formed a structure around the lock, and the spider maneuvered between and round the threads like an artist at an easel. Slowly, he drew the magic aside like a curtain, leaving the lock bare.

Olga watched in wonder. "Your magic . . . ," she said, "it's more than illusions. You can move things, change things."

"As will you. Together our magic can break this curse."

What had seemed to Olga an impossible task was the work of a moment with her friends beside her. She had never been one to ask for help, fearing that no one would come to her aid. But now in her hour of need, her friends had come.

The spider stood on the heavy handle. "I did the magic," he said. "But I think opening the door is beyond me."

Olga wanted to laugh, but she was worried about making any noise. So instead, she placed her fingers on the handle and turned.

It clanked open.

twenty-two

A figure moved in the shadows, and Olga nearly screamed. A hand covered her mouth, followed by a voice hurriedly whispering, "It's me!"

Pavel! "Don't scare me like that!" she hissed.

"Never thought I could scare you." He flashed a smile that she could barely make out in the gloomy stairwell. He caught sight of Pauk on Olga's shoulder and fought back a shudder. "Your spider's friendly," he said with forced brightness.

Before she could give him a tart reply, he grabbed her arm and led her down the corridor.

"Where are we going?" she whispered.

He held up a finger, shushing her.

Together they darted through the palace, until at last he opened a door and Olga slipped into the room beyond. He closed the door with quiet care behind them.

They were in the music room. The instruments lining the walls seemed to give off a soft hum, the wood warm and inviting in the cold morning light. Of course Pavel would want to come here.

"What if they find us?" she asked.

Pavel shook his head. "The room was covered in dust when we searched here before, and it was the same when I found it again. I wonder if it was only ever used by his wife."

For a moment Olga wasn't sure if the floor had wobbled or if she had merely stumbled. His wife. Her mother. Her mother had come here, and these would have been her instruments.

Memories filled her, seizing her heart in an iron grip. There were songs that her mother would croon on winter nights in front of the fire, in summer out under the stars, her voice lilting and dancing through the air to lull Olga to sleep. Olga placed careful fingers on one of the instruments, too softly to make a sound but enough to feel memories pulsing through the strings. She could sense her mother here. A mother she hardly remembered, but who was a part of her.

Pavel was watching her in silence. He was her family too. Olga blinked back tears. She felt so ashamed, like a failure. Everything about her plan had gone wrong, and worst of all, she had lied to him, and possibly ruined his chances of happiness with Anna. He wasn't supposed to come back for her. If Pavel had followed Mr. Bulgakov's way of thinking—Olga's way of thinking—he would have left Olga behind. Yet he had come in search of her.

"You rescued me," said Olga, and it wasn't a thank-you, even though she knew it should have been. Instead, it was something sour, a pathetic truth that she didn't want to admit and would prefer to forget. She wanted to ask why, but instead, she said, "How?" She hadn't thought he would be able to find her.

Pavel's forehead wrinkled in concentration. "It's strange, but there's something that I could feel. Like a string tying us at each end. And somehow I knew that if I followed it, it would lead me to you."

Now it was Olga's turn to be confused. She wasn't aware of any magic she had done. Stranger still that Pavel could feel it, was able to follow it. Maybe it was something stronger than magic. A truth she didn't quite understand. Whatever it was, she was grateful.

"Thank you for coming to save me," she said. She hadn't been able to bring herself to say the words until now.

Pavel looked at her in surprise. "I don't think I've ever heard you thank me for anything before," he said, smiling.

She couldn't quite meet his gaze. He had always been the one who waited for her, who came back for her, and she had repaid him with lies.

She sat down on the piano bench, motioning for him to sit beside her.

"I have to tell you something."

Pavel stared at his hands, his knuckles white. "So you're saying . . . Anna loves me? It was you who said those awful things?"

"Yes," said Olga, staring at her own hands, still afraid to meet his eyes. "And I believe Anna does." She took a deep breath. It was possible the next thing that she had to say to him would break her own heart. "I'm grateful you came back. You saved me, and I want to repay you by letting you be happy. You should go to her."

A furrow creased Pavel's brow. "You think I would just leave you?" he said. "Because I've found someone new?"

"Not someone new—someone better," she said, her voice tight. "Someone who cares about others and treats them with kindness, and likes music, and stories, and—"

Pavel cut her off. "Olga, I would never—"

"You were going to run away with Anna!" Olga cried. She bit back a sob. She'd spent so long feeling unwanted. Now the memory of that conversation with Pavel in the garden left behind only hurt.

"No, no, no . . . ," said Pavel. "I wanted us to run away together. *All* of us." There was truth in his eyes, but she struggled to believe him.

She remembered their fight. They'd never argued before coming to this horrible palace. "You said I think only of myself. That I don't trust anyone. And then I pretended to be the person you love. I wouldn't blame you if you hate me."

Pavel took her shoulders in his hands, turning her to face him. "But, Olga, I love you too. You believe me, right?" he said. "That won't go away just because I met Anna. My love for her is different, but it doesn't mean I love you less."

"Aren't you mad at me for lying to you?" she said.

"Oh, I am. It was terrible, what you did," said Pavel. Then he gave a pained half smile as he added, "But there are people we need to help, and it will be much harder to break the curse if we're not speaking to each other." He paused a moment, thoughtful. "Are you sorry? Truly?"

"More than anything. I shouldn't have hurt you."

"Then we can figure out the rest later." He clapped a hand on her back. "For now, we need a plan."

Gratitude filled her stomach, food for a hunger that she'd tried very hard to ignore. But soon her thoughts shifted to excitement, for something Pavel said had given her an idea.

She touched her hand to his, while the other hovered just over her heartstring. "I think I know how we can save the others," she said.

"Pauk taught me that I could use my magic little by little. I could do spells I would never have been able to pull off without getting sick or tired." Excitement burned inside Olga as she and Pavel stalked down the corridor from the music room. "But what we need to do is meld the magic with another object to make something new."

From his new perch on Pavel's shoulder, the spider beamed as Olga explained what she'd learned.

"I think we need to sew something. A cloak, a tunic, a dress—I can sew my magic into it to craft a new spell, something that will overpower the baron's."

Even Pauk shivered with excitement as he listened to Olga's idea. "The sewing room."

Olga nodded. "If we can get to the sewing room, I can find enough fabric for a spell to help the others. And I know someone who will help us." She gave a small bow to Pauk. "After the sewing room, we must go to the woods."

As she said this, a bell tolled midday. Voices surged, and rattling footsteps stomped down a nearby corridor in a rhythmic march.

Olga and Pavel froze. Pavel reached for the handle of a nearby door, slowly and silently. More footsteps, closer this time. Olga tiptoed toward the door, holding her breath. Together they prepared to slip inside.

But the soldiers didn't turn down their hall, and soon the steps grew steadily fainter until they disappeared entirely.

"How are we supposed to get to the other side of the palace," said Pavel, "without one of them spotting us?"

"This is going to be more dangerous than I thought," Olga said.

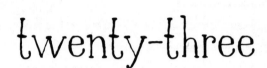

twenty-three

They needed disguises that would help them elude the notice of the soldiers. But there wasn't time for an elaborate plan.

"What are you thinking?" asked Pavel once they'd returned to the music room.

Olga was assessing his clothes, looking for something she could take apart and remake quickly. "Your sash," she said.

He unwrapped it from his waist and handed it to her. The crimson silk was slippery in her hands. This had to be another item gifted from the baron.

"It's lovely," she said. "So please forgive me for what I'm about to do."

Pavel winced as she ripped the fabric lengthwise, tearing it into long strips. Then she set to work, braiding the strips together along with a strand of her magic to form a long cord that could be tied as a belt. She did the same with fabric torn from the hem of her shirt.

"Lift your arms," she commanded. Pavel did as she asked, and Olga wrapped one of the cords around his waist.

"It's nicer this way," Pavel said admiringly. "The sash was too much."

Olga tied the ends into a practical, if not elegant, knot. The magic hummed against her fingers as the spell expanded, spreading at the pace of a wildfire over Pavel's torso, up to his hair, out to his fingers. It wasn't enough to make him fully invisible, but the cord shimmered, offering Pavel a powerful camouflage. He became candlelight and stone walls. Olga tied her own belt around her waist. When finished, she peered at her arms and saw only shadows. The braiding was rushed and sloppy, the ends jagged, but the magic worked.

Much as Olga would have loved to delay their plans, she knew there wasn't much time. If anyone had delivered food to the crypt, they would have found Olga missing, and the baron was likely to begin using the soldiers for his own aims as early as the ball that evening.

They crept through unused corridors, Pavel expertly leading the way to avoid detection.

Every direction they went, the rooms and hallways were teeming with soldiers. The rooms that had been vacant on Olga and Pavel's arrival were alive with booming voices and hands slapping playing cards.

On the right was a series of open arches revealing the shelves and tables of a library. The laughter and conversation of dozens of voices resounded from within. Olga and Pavel hovered by the nearest arch, mere feet away from a soldier they could hear but couldn't see.

"They'll see us," Olga whispered.

"They won't. Your magic is working," Pavel said. Somehow he managed to stay upbeat even when arguing.

"Then they'll hear us."

"Then stop talking. And step lightly."

He took a step forward, then another. Olga had to squint to catch glimpses of him so she could mimic his steps. She didn't allow herself to breathe.

Soldiers slouching in cozy chairs dotted the library like mushrooms. Others were gathered at tables playing games. Pebbles clinked on a wooden game board while onlookers laughed and cheered. None of them turned or shouted at the figures slipping past the archways.

After turning the corner, Olga allowed herself a breath.

"Pavel was right," said Pauk, and there was pride in his voice.

"About what?" she said.

"Your magic is working."

But Olga shook her head. As eager as she was to set their plans in motion, seeds of doubt had started to sprout. "It's still only an illusion. I've never made something real."

"We will together. My queen has confidence in your skills, and I trust her."

He sounded so certain that Olga found she was starting to believe him.

Somehow they made it through the labyrinthine hallways and approached the servants' wing. Between them and the door was a large room. A group of soldiers had chosen this place to congregate, the clink of their tankards and rumble of their laughter echoing down the corridor.

The trio watched in stunned silence. They'd made it this far, but if the door to the servants' wing was closed, opening it without attracting the notice of soldiers mere feet away was impossible.

"We can't just wait around all afternoon," said Olga. "We're going to have to get past them." She half expected Pavel to disagree, but instead, he reached and took her arm, giving it a squeeze of reassurance.

"I'll lead," he said. "They can fight me if they see me."

"There must be twenty soldiers there!" Pauk exclaimed from Pavel's shoulder.

"You'd be outnumbered a dozen to one," said Olga. "But your bravery is noted." She looked toward the wall on their right. The doors to the garden stood open, letting a warm breeze sweep through the space, bringing with it a hint of rose petals and the coming autumn's dry leaves. "If we go through the gardens, I can climb through the window."

There was something comforting and familiar about the idea. Mr. Bulgakov's plans had often involved Olga climbing through windows while Pavel stood guard. Together they tiptoed toward the doors, following a sculpted staircase down into the quiet and still air.

They traced a path that ran parallel to the palace walls, following it until at last they spied a window. It was more than two floors up, but at least it was next to a trellis.

"Is that anywhere near the sewing room?" Pavel asked.

"That will be another floor up, I think," said Olga, noting that the trellis stopped too short for her to climb the full way to the third floor. "But once I'm in the second-floor corridor, there will be stairs nearby."

"Do you want me to come with you?" Pavel asked.

"Better you keep watch."

"I'll wait near the entrance hall," said Pavel. He gave her shoulder a squeeze. After that, he was so quiet, and the magic disguising him so effective, that it took a moment for Olga to realize that he had gone.

Silently, she grabbed the vines and brambles that clung to the trellis. She nearly cried out as the bark and thorns stung her hands, but she clamped her mouth tight and pulled herself up. The trellis moved under her weight and leaves rustled. Olga froze, trying to keep her breaths shallow. When she began climbing again, her movements were smoother, and any sway of the leaves would have been difficult to attribute to anything other than a breeze.

Until her foot slipped. Olga yelped as she dangled, hovering high enough off the ground that she wondered whether to call for Pavel to catch her. But no, soldiers would surely come running then. She gritted her teeth and managed to grab the trellis with her other hand. A few more steps and she'd hauled herself up to the window, then pried it open, slipping through into a shadowy room. All was silent here.

She made her way across the floor toward an entrance that she hoped would lead to a corridor. The door creaked a little as she swung it open.

"Who's there?" called a voice, and Olga stiffened. Holding her breath, she dared not move.

A soldier stepped forward at a far end of the corridor. "Is someone here?" he called out. He was looking at the door but could not see Olga standing beside it. She felt a tingle of excitement that her magic was working so well.

"Show yourself, spirit!" the soldier shouted. He waited, watching.

Olga shifted, slipping through the door and into the shadows. She paused, checking whether he'd heard her, but he hadn't moved. Quietly, she backed away from him, and the soldier did not follow her as she climbed the nearby stairs to the sewing room.

It was easy to duck inside. This room was empty except for the enormous shelves filled with bolts of beautiful fabric.

She sought a fabric that was light enough to carry but plentiful enough for dozens of people. She walked through the

stacks, touching each one, feeling its weight, searching for a material that was sufficient to do what she needed.

A glimmer on a low shelf caught her eye, and Olga reached to withdraw a white fabric interwoven with silvery threads and soft as goose down. She lifted the bolt, and it was light enough for her to carry. This would do.

It was a complete bolt. No one had ever used it before. She wondered if it had been purchased for her mother, for a dress that would never be worn. Or perhaps even for herself. Olga suddenly thought of all the fancy dresses she might have worn. How different her life would have been. Less hunger, less sadness, less struggle. But no Pavel. And the baron as her father. This last thought made her pause—she couldn't bring herself to think of loving him, but she also couldn't help wondering what he would have been like if things had gone differently.

And Olga—would she have been a different person if she hadn't had to fight and steal and swindle? And maybe . . . maybe her mother wouldn't have gotten sick.

But these were questions that couldn't be answered. The ache would always be there, the scars of what she'd endured. She couldn't change what had happened, but she could decide what would happen next.

Olga wrapped an end of her belt around the bolt so that the magic she'd crafted to conceal herself could mask it too.

She'd come to this palace searching for treasure. But she could now see plain as day that the chance to save the others was worth far more than gold.

twenty-four

As Olga climbed back down the trellis to the garden, a swan peeked out at her from its hiding place in the shrubbery. It watched her with onyx eyes.

She stepped forward, clutching the bolt of fabric she'd taken from the palace in one hand and quietly raising the other in a gesture of greeting and compassion. The danger of what was facing the swans pressed in on her.

The swan blinked, and she recognized the dark pattern around its head, the curve of its neck. She'd met this swan before. It stared at her with an almost-human curiosity. She'd met the swan, but had she met its human form too?

Suddenly she couldn't bring herself to leave this swan behind. She stepped closer, and the bird jerked away from her, skittish as a baby fawn.

But Olga, with slow careful steps, kept moving closer, trying to get near enough to whisper to it. She knelt, hoping the swan would understand that Olga wasn't a danger. That somehow her intent would reach the person inside.

"Come with me," she breathed. "Come with me."

The swan moved closer, as if it wanted to hear, to understand her words. She murmured over and over, almost a chant, and soon the swan was close to her, in the middle of the path. Exposed.

Olga heard the arrow before it landed. The bird let out a screech as it slumped to the ground.

A soldier stood at the end of the path. He still didn't seem to see her, but he did see the swan he'd felled. He looked at it disappointedly before he muttered to himself, "Just a normal swan. Not one of those creatures after all." He stepped forward to retrieve his arrow, yanking it from the bird and wiping the dripping scarlet from its tip before replacing it in his quiver. Then he made to return to his post.

Fury burned through Olga. The stolen fabric tumbling from her arms, she held out a palm, ripping a strand of magic from herself and lashing it at the man. It crackled through the air, binding his arms and legs in an instant. He fell to the ground hard, a look of shock and wonder on his face. He had no idea what had just happened to him or who was behind it.

Olga collapsed to her knees beside the swan, reeling from the use of so much magic. Giving herself a second to catch her breath, she began to search the swan for the wound. It was near the base of the wing—the arrow hadn't pierced its chest. Painful, though not deadly. But she couldn't leave the poor thing like this.

"Pavel, come quick," she hissed in the direction of the entrance hall.

There was a gentle rustling as he crept down the path to crouch beside her.

"We have to get this swan out of here," she said. "It's hurt."

And Pavel didn't need any further explanation. "You take the fabric"—he nodded to where the smuggled fabric lay on the ground nearby—"and run. I'll follow behind."

"But they'll see you," said Olga.

"I know," said Pavel. "That's why you have to go first. It'll be okay," he added, and she almost believed him.

With a final moment of hesitation, Olga turned, choosing to trust him, even when logic told her that there was now no chance of escape. She grabbed the fabric and quickly moved to one of the narrower garden paths. The commotion had started to attract more soldiers, whose footsteps were drawing nearer.

This path twisted, and more than once she had to double back. A lawn stretched out before her, separating her from the gate, but there were no soldiers in her way, and she stumbled

across it, her breaths labored, her movements sluggish. She paused as she grasped the gate handle, waiting, searching behind her for a glimpse of Pavel.

Soldiers stood at the far end of the lawn. They weren't chasing Olga—their focus was entirely on some disturbance on one of the hedged paths. Chatter rippled through the group, and several soldiers drew their weapons.

Soon Olga understood their confusion. Approaching was the strange sight of a limp swan floating above the path, as if by magic. For though Pavel was invisible to them, the swan he carried was not.

"What is that?" cried one of the soldiers.

"Something's wrong with it. It doesn't look right. Is it flying?"

"It's been hurt already," another said. "Look, it's bleeding."

"We should just let it die."

"No. We need to finish it off," a soldier declared, and stepping confidently toward the swan, he withdrew a dagger from his belt. Then he abruptly lurched back as the invisible Pavel used his strength to push the soldier away.

"What the—?" said the soldier, seeing only the floating swan, not Pavel.

The other men became agitated. One of the soldiers clawed at Pavel, managing to rip the threads of his shirt. The belt tore. It broke the magic concealing him, and he appeared before them in a burst of light and shadow.

"A demon," the soldiers gasped.

"No, it's just an illusion," said another. "Get him!"

But Pavel was faster, and he darted around them.

A shout burst from Olga. "Hurry!"

Pavel was catching up to her, but the soldiers were gaining on him. "Run!" he shouted.

She did, turning and crashing through the gate. She could hear the shouts of soldiers as Pavel raced behind her. Heavy boots dislodged soil and rocks as others joined the chase.

Olga managed to scramble into the shelter of the nearby trees, but a branch snagged her belt, and the magic concealing her flickered. They were both visible now. As Pavel neared, Olga snatched his hand. Withdrawing another strand of magic, she threw it around them, making both of them—and the swan—fully invisible once more.

The soldiers paused, unseeing.

"Where did they go?" shouted one. "They were just here."

"They must be farther ahead."

And soon the soldiers who had followed were passing them, searching for a path that didn't exist.

But Olga could hear no more. She'd used too much of her magic, and the world began to swirl around her. Knees buckling, she sank to the ground. Her head spun, and faintness claimed her.

Beneath her, the earth rumbled. Somewhere in the valley, another rockslide was reshaping the landscape.

The warmth of a blanket tickled Olga's face. She brushed her fingers over it and realized it wasn't a blanket at all—it was a web. For a moment she fought back a scream, convinced this was some sort of nightmare and a monster was about to eat her. But then her eyes adjusted and she began to recognize her surroundings. She was in Mokosh's cave.

Pavel sat nearby, holding a stick and roasting something savory over the fire.

"How—how did we get here?" she asked. Pavel had never met Mokosh before. He could never have found the cave on his own.

"My loyal subject led him here," said Mokosh, amusement curling in her voice as she glanced at Pauk on her wrist. The ancient woman moved toward Olga with her strange spidery gait and lowered herself onto one of the chairs nearby. A handful of spiders skittered over her.

Pavel flinched at the sight of so many scuttling legs but chose not to mention any unease. "You used too much of your magic," he said instead. It wasn't an accusation; there was gratitude in his voice.

"I know," said Olga, rubbing her head. She felt better now—she must have been asleep awhile. "How long has it been?"

"A few hours."

The words reminded Olga of *why* she had overspent her magic. What she had been doing. . . .

"Where is the swan?"

Pavel motioned to a webbed cushion where the swan slept, its wing bandaged.

"And the fabric?" Olga asked. "Did it come back with us?"

Mokosh nodded and pointed toward the cave wall, where

the bolt leaned next to Pavel's domra. But the spider queen didn't take her eyes from Olga. "What made you change your mind?" she asked. There was no resentment in her tone.

Olga winced at the memory of the angry words she had hurled at Mokosh the last time she'd been in this cave. There was too much to explain, too many painful emotions that had led her to this new desire to help break the curse. She tried to keep her voice light as she shrugged. "You were right."

The spider queen's eyes narrowed, and Olga knew that the ancient woman was seeing through the protective layers she'd always tried to wrap around herself. Understanding passed between them.

"I want to do better," Olga added quietly. "To use my heartstring for a cause that's worthy of its power."

"And the valley?"

"It's my home too. And I'm going to fight to save it." Olga's voice tremored a little, but she allowed it. The thought of facing the baron—her father—frightened her, yet it was a fear worth facing.

Mokosh gave a sharp nod. "Then let us begin."

The spider queen's powers had faded from their former glory. But she was able to offer instruction, guiding Olga on how to develop and focus the intent behind her spellwork. Olga's satchel had fortunately made the trip back from the palace, and she withdrew one of the needles and pulled a fine thread through it.

"It's the same as Pauk showed you," said the spider queen. "You must speak your purpose to the magic as you craft it. It will flow from you, and from there you can guide it."

Olga fumbled as she gathered a length of the fabric, and Pavel rushed to her side to help her. At first, she wanted to shoo him away. But there was a relief in finding that someone was beside her, someone she could lean on if her hands grew weak or if she stumbled. So she said nothing.

They quickly realized that there wasn't enough fabric in the bolt Olga had stolen from the palace to make clothes for all the guests. Olga buried her face in her hands, feeling foolish.

"It won't matter," said Mokosh reassuringly. "The intent determines the spell, not how much magic you use."

Still, they needed to make enough for dozens of people.

"You could make a sash or belt, like you made before," suggested Pauk.

"It can be simple," added Mokosh, "so long as your heart-string helps to craft something new."

"What about a kerchief to tie around their necks? It will look very dashing," chirped Pavel. "And perhaps I can have one when you're finished? It's such a nice fabric. It's difficult to tie the more fashionable knots unless you have something this fine."

Olga fought the urge to glare at him, but with Mokosh and Pauk's added encouragement, she finally, albeit reluctantly, agreed that smaller squares of fabric were their best chance at making enough for everyone.

For this swan, though, she still wanted to sew something special. She was sure it was the swan who had helped her in the aviary. So she snipped pieces of the fabric to form the pattern of a swan-sized cloak that could act as a shawl for a human, and without another word she set to work.

Her hands flew, hardly feeling the flowing fabric beneath her fingers, the needle sliding effortlessly through woven threads. The small strand of her magic blended with her stitches, making the whole of the fabric vibrate with her spell. The cloak began to take shape, silvery as moonlight, soft and sweeping. It would be a lovely garment.

As she tied the last knot, Olga gathered the cloak in her arms.

Mokosh's watchful eyes were unwavering as Olga crossed the cave toward the resting swan. This was the moment for Olga to prove she had learned how to use her magic properly.

She approached the swan and threw the cloak over it. The fabric clung to its body.

Olga closed her eyes and held her breath, willing the magic to do as she'd intended.

Seconds, then minutes, passed. The swan didn't change. Olga had hoped that her magic would be enough. That she was enough. She shrank back, dispirited.

"I can't do it. I'm like the baron—I can only do magic when it tricks or hurts people."

But Mokosh shook her head, the jittery movement so similar to that of her subjects. "No, that's not true." The spiders clustered on her arm seemed to nod in agreement. "When I gifted that first strand, it was meant to channel the heart's truest desires. The baron has twisted it into something else, but you will return magic to what it was."

But Olga hardly heard her. "I'm not powerful enough," she said.

"You are," Pauk protested.

Still Olga ignored their words of encouragement. Her mind was a whirring clockwork as she analyzed the pieces of her spell. She spoke her thoughts aloud. "What if there is something to be learned from the baron's curse?"

The others murmured, uncertain, but Olga's thoughts were racing. She'd remembered what the baron had given her, and what was inside it. Quickly, she rummaged through her satchel, withdrawing the locket. She pried open the clasp, and the heartstring inside tumbled onto her outstretched palm.

"My mother's heartstring," she said. "If the baron can use the heartstrings of others to strengthen his spells, then perhaps I could use hers. She would want to break this curse—she'd be horrified to know what he's done."

Snipping only a pinch of the strand, Olga twisted it with her own heartstring. The combined thread slipped easily through the eye of her needle. It would be enough to add only a couple of stitches, but if it was anything like the magic she'd done in the forest, that would suffice. With the thread, she embroidered a tiny flower near the cloak's collar. When the last petal was complete, Olga draped the fabric over the swan once more. It cascaded over the bird in flowing waves.

The air shifted in an instant, buzzing with the energy of a lightning strike. Before their eyes the fabric had begun to pulse, glowing brighter with each new heartbeat.

Beneath the draped fabric, feathers smoothed to skin, legs lengthened. The wings became delicate arms. This was nothing like the sunset transformation Olga had witnessed at the lakeshore. Back then, the swans had seemed to writhe, their shift to human form painful. Now it was more akin to sunlight bursting through clouds after a storm. The swan form fading away, the human emerging from the dissolving mist.

The figure was crouched, waist-length black tresses hiding the face like curtains. But when a trembling hand brushed the hair aside, it was Anna's face that greeted them. She snatched a sharp breath, tense with apparent shock at finding people surrounding her in an unfamiliar place. But her eyes took in Pavel and Olga, then welled with tears.

For a moment, Olga worried that she'd done wrong. Anna had welcomed her curse. Olga remembered how Anna had longed to be beautiful, had worried that no one would love her without the baron's magic. And in looking at the real Anna, Olga could see that she did look different. Her hair was a touch less lustrous, her skin less dewy, her lips smaller. But it was still Anna. The beauty of her kind heart shone in the twinkle of her eyes and the warmth of her beaming smile.

Olga was about to re-

assure her when Anna leaned forward and wrapped her arms around Pavel. "You're here," she said, her face buried in Pavel's shoulder. She squeezed her eyes shut, but the tears slipped through and trickled onto Pavel's waistcoat.

From the mouth of the cave, Olga felt the ground tremble. In the surrounding mountains, smashing echoed as a rockslide tumbled into one of the valley's many ravines. The valley was waiting for them to end the curse, but it seemed its patience was wearing thin.

She had retreated outside, wanting to give Anna and Pavel a private moment. He needed time to explain how he'd intended to declare his love at the ball that night, and their happiness would bloom like rosebuds. Olga tried to remind herself of what Pavel had said—that him loving Anna didn't mean Olga would be left alone.

A twig snapped, and Olga turned.

"May I join you?" asked Anna. She gestured to the far end of the log on which Olga sat, and since Olga didn't protest, Anna seated herself on it. "Pavel told me . . . ," she began, but she didn't speak further. Instead, a thick silence settled between them.

All the things Olga wanted to say felt small and insubstantial, like silt filtering between open fingers. She wanted to say that Anna would be right to take Pavel away, that Olga deserved to be alone. But that would be making this about herself, and she'd done enough of that already. She knew there was a chance Anna wouldn't forgive her, and she would have to understand that. "I'm so sorry," she said meekly.

"I wanted to be your friend," Anna whispered. It was painful hearing Anna speak with such reserve.

"I know," said Olga. "Pavel told me once that I do a poor job of trusting people. He was right." She stared at her hands, at the calluses on her fingers, the scars from scrapes and cuts she'd acquired during Mr. Bulgakov's many schemes.

"There's a story I read once," Anna said, betraying a touch of giddiness, like the Anna from the ballroom, "about a girl who was approached by a bear. The secret was that the bear was actually a prince in disguise. She was frightened—I know I would be! Can you imagine something so giant, with such claws? But when she learned to trust him, the bearskin fell away."

"Are you saying I should befriend bears?"

At this, Anna did laugh, even though her cheeks were glistening with tears. "I think you're not alone in being frightened." She gave a sigh.

"Aren't you afraid I might hurt you or Pavel again?" Olga asked. She quickly added, "I want to do better."

To Olga's surprise, Anna scooted nearer to her, close enough to take Olga's hand in her own. "I found this valley because I had a wish. And even though it went wrong, I can't regret wishing," Anna said softly, and Olga had to admire the way that Anna found a brightness in everything, even a curse. "If I looked only at how things are, I'd miss out on imagining what they could become."

Olga heard the hope in Anna's words, and she finally

understood. Anna was trusting that Olga wouldn't hurt her again, and that trust was precious. She had a chance to take a new path, to find a new way forward. It reminded her of when she'd stood at the top of the valley—she'd believed coming here was the start of a new life. And it had been, just not in the way she'd expected.

She hadn't truly wanted the jewel; she'd wanted the freedom that came with it. But the others in the palace didn't have that option—not yet. They were still trapped as Anna had been, in danger of losing themselves forever.

The weight of what Olga had to do pressed on her. And as her worries grew, the valley itself seemed to cry ever more desperately for help. Once again the ground shuddered and shook, nearly knocking Olga off her seat. She waited until the rumbling stopped. This had to end now.

Returning to the palace would place her in even more danger. But for the first time, Olga found it wasn't herself she was worried about.

The Spider Spins
His Final Tale

Why do I tell you these stories, little ones? Of humans, and swans, and how these tales interweave with our own spider histories?

I could tell you the story of a spider who saw it all. Who observed these people and knew them. But I don't like to speak of myself. And so I tell you what I saw.

Because you know what happened and how it led to where you are now—you can predict what will come next. But until now, you did not know those involved as I knew them, their fears and hopes and sorrows. It is easy to think of them as heroes and villains, to wonder at them, to scoff at how they differ from yourselves. It is tempting to think of how you would have chosen differently.

But the people I speak of did not have the advantage of seeing their stories as we do. They were finding their way through a dark forest, seeing each other, perceiving only what was closest to them. They stumbled. They fought. And ultimately, they triumphed.

Your stories are still ahead of you. I hope that when you see a strand before you, you will remember what I've told you. And if you are presented with a similar choice, I hope that you will make the right one.

The right choice, little ones, is what you must decide for yourselves.

twenty-five

K nowing they had a spell that worked—that there was truly a way to break this curse—gave a new bustle of urgency to everyone in the cave. The late-summer sunset was steadily approaching, and they needed to leave the cave in time to trek to the lakeshore. Pavel worked to cut strips of fabric, with Anna drawing on the skills she'd gained in her years as a seamstress. She was more adept with a needle than Olga, and she gave both of her friends guidance to help them work faster. The spiders skittering along the cave floor carried spools of thread, needles, and berries and mushrooms foraged from the forest to support them as they toiled. Some of the spiders even helped with the sewing, their tiny hands hooking threads through the soft cloth.

The heartstring in Olga's hands slipped out of the needle again, and she growled in frustration. "If only we had a spinning wheel," she cried. It would be a faster way of weaving her mother's heartstring together with hers using real thread. She'd been trying to twist the threads together by hand, but they kept unraveling in her haste.

A mischievous grin slanted across Mokosh's face. "I think I can help you with that."

The spiders in the room dispersed, leaving the cave strangely empty without their constant wriggling movements. Before Olga had a chance to ask what they were doing, they returned carrying bits of wood. Together the swarm moved like a black cloud, shifting pieces into place and tying them together with webbing. After a moment the spiders moved aside, and a crude spinning wheel stood where there had been nothing just before.

"Whoa," Pavel said, speaking Olga's thoughts aloud. "That was so incredible, and so disgusting."

Olga couldn't have said it better.

She wasn't great at spinning—they hadn't exactly had room in Mr. Bulgakov's cart to carry a spinning wheel around—but she knew the basics. Taking a step toward it, she was stopped by a spindly outstretched arm.

"Let me," said Mokosh, swelling with pride. "If there's one thing I know well, it's how to spin thread." She took the strands from Olga and seated herself beside the wheel. "My magic might be at rest," she said, and a fire burned in her eyes. "But it looks like this way I can do one last spell."

All working together, it took every hour remaining until sunset to craft the kerchiefs needed for so many guests. Each time they stopped to question whether they had enough, they continued, certain that the baron had already begun to use the soldiers' heartstrings. As afternoon fell into early evening, they knew that they could wait no longer. Bundling all their finished pieces in aching arms, the group assembled to begin their journey down the mountain to the palace.

There was a moment of surprise when Mokosh made movements to join them.

"What if the baron sees you?" asked Olga. "If he harmed you, what would it do to the valley?"

"We want to protect you," added Pavel.

"I'm elderly and fragile, you mean," said Mokosh. It was difficult to tell whether she was annoyed or amused.

Even the spiders seemed to murmur their concern for their queen.

The old woman said sharply, "I'm here to save this valley, and I'm not confining myself to this cave while you do it on your own." There was so much command in her spidery frame that the others had no choice but to agree.

She did move surprisingly swiftly for an ancient immortal being. With the kerchiefs gathered, Pavel led them over roots and around craggy slopes, navigating to cut the quickest path down the hillside. Twigs scratched their faces and moss was slippery under their feet. But the longer they walked, the more the valley seemed to make way for them. Dry paths opened out before them, and overhead the *chack chack* of thrushes and the *puu puu* of cuckoos cheered them on.

At last the palace was visible through the trees, its candlelight already glaring through the windows. The sun behind it painted the turrets with an orange light. The stone walls

stood impenetrable, as though the baron knew they were coming and had sought to seal his home off like a fortress. From within, orders could be heard from captains to their soldiers.

Suddenly the thought of seeing her father—meeting him for the first time with full awareness of who he was—made Olga's hands tremble. She clutched the kerchiefs tight to her chest, trying to breathe.

Pavel was the first to notice, and he took Olga's shoulders in his hands. "Your work is done," he said gently. "We can handle things from here if you wish to stay hidden."

But Olga bit her lip and shook her head. She wanted to see this through, to unravel the magic herself. To undo what she'd done.

The sun, reigning from its mountain throne, threatened to blind them with its radiance. A sharp wind swept past the wall, snatching at leaves and at the fabric they carried.

With more bravery than she felt, Olga took a step forward. Once she might have tried to face this alone, but now, as her knees trembled from nerves and from the use of so much magic, she was grateful to have her friends beside her.

Together, they traced the wall toward the lakeshore. Just over the stone wall, the soldiers' voices were harsh and alert.

When Olga reached the wall's corner, the lake stretched out, filling the valley with a fiery glow. Its waters rippled in the wind. The swans had already gathered, their feathers ruffled, their agitated honks splitting the air. The baron's curse meant that they could become human once more when the sun fell, but if Olga and her friends could move quickly, they would ensure that the people gathered would become their human selves forever.

It was Pavel who approached the first swan. He sang a low and soothing tune, reaching with gentle fingers outstretched. He stepped into the water, his boot squelching in the mud. The nearby swan watched him, curious, its beady black eyes wary. But Pavel was swift, and with a single movement he withdrew a kerchief from his stash and looped it around the swan's neck, pulling the ends into a swift knot.

The swan floated, unmoving. As seconds stretched past, Olga worried that she'd used too little magic, that they had done their work too hastily. But then the swan began to shift and transform, feathers molting, human eyes blinking from a reshaping face. Water cascaded from its growing figure, until at last a human stood before them.

Pavel knew this person, greeting him by name and shaking his hand, and Olga was ashamed to realize how long she had been in the palace without learning anything of the others who were captive here.

There was no pop or explosion of fireworks, but all at once it felt as though the spell was broken. Not simply the baron's spells on the people here, but a spell that Olga had been under her whole life. Looking out for herself wasn't enough anymore. Simply surviving wasn't enough.

Breaking the curse, seeing these people free of its weight, that was enough. Learning to use her magic was enough. Feeling wanted was enough.

Quickly, she and Anna followed Pavel's example, approaching the swans and placing the kerchiefs around their necks. One by one the birds transformed, regaining their human shape. And as more humans appeared and recognized what was happening, they too joined in helping the others. Shouts filled the air, and people hugged and laughed with delight even as they slipped in mud and shivered in their wet clothes. Olga took in their faces: the round woman with her broad smile and hair the color of molasses. The angular man with his trim black beard, offering his cloak to an elderly woman. One of the twins calling for his brother. Everywhere there was joy and fear and pain, real people emerging at last. Gone was that illusion so carefully curated by the baron.

OooEEEaaaooo. A low cry floated from the trees. Olga turned toward the forest to see the creatures emerging, eyes aglow. A wave of alarm rippled through the crowd, and people clutched at one another as the monsters drew close.

"Wh-what are they?" asked Anna as Pavel wrapped a protective arm around her.

Olga shared a glance with Mokosh. They knew there was nothing to fear. These were no wild beasts, they were simply humans seeking an end to their own curse.

"The baron did this. They were swans too, but when his magic began to fail, he imprisoned them as these creatures."

Extending her hand as Pavel had done with the swans, Olga approached them, clucking in as soothing a tone as she could muster. One stood ahead of the others, whether to assert itself as leader or protect the others in its cursed flock, she wasn't sure. It was the leader she approached, giving a respectful bow as she held out the kerchief for its inspection.

The creature inched closer, its eyes focused on the cloth in her hands. It sniffed. A tongue jabbed between its fangs and tasted the air. At last it bowed, and Olga gently wrapped the kerchief around its neck and secured it with a tight knot.

An eerie silence fell in spite of the commotion and chaos happening amongst the humans and swans behind her. Olga was breathless as she waited for the magic to take hold, for the monster to be freed of its cage.

But nothing changed. There was no hum of magic in the air surrounding it. No trembling of its skin to signify a transformation.

Her heart sank.

Mokosh placed a hand on Olga's shoulder.

"What's happened?" Olga said. "What's gone wrong?"

"Something's missing," Mokosh replied. And from the worry in her voice, it was clear that she didn't know the answer either.

Olga wanted to howl in frustration and despair. These people were still trapped, and she didn't know how to save them.

The words Mokosh had uttered in the cave hung over Olga, teasing her. The strongest magic came from a full heart. The baron had said something similar. Her heart wasn't strong enough for this magic.

"I see my lost witch has returned," the baron's voice rang out.

Olga's blood ran cold at the sound of that voice. Her father. The man who had caused so much pain. She was drawn to him, and she hated him. She was hungry for him to recognize her, furious at him for using people like tools to be discarded.

He stood on the crest of the hill, his cloak billowing behind him, his white hair flaming in the light of the sunset. He strutted from his high position, but it was not Olga he approached. Instead, he launched himself toward one of the palace guests and snatched at the kerchief, yanking it from around her neck. It fluttered down, and he ground it beneath his boot.

"You think your little spells will save them?" he snapped. "I will shred them. One by one."

There was a painful splintering inside Olga. "You have no idea what you just did," she seethed. She didn't know if ripping the fabric was enough to break the spell she'd made, but she did know that the kerchief held her mother's heartstring. The only precious piece of her mother remaining. And he was stomping on it like an insect. He was a fiend. A monster.

"Consider me unconcerned," he said, but though his words seemed nonchalant, there was a boiling anger beneath. He withdrew a handkerchief from his own pocket and wiped his hands with it as though her spells had dirtied him. His breaths were heavy, his disgust masking his fury.

The sun sank below the horizon, and suddenly the illusions surrounding him were bright and clear. Hardly anything remained of the threads he'd wrapped around himself, exposing the scales of his corrupted form.

Low growls echoed. The creatures closed in on him, their eyes glowing, their claws scraping through the dirt.

But the baron wasn't watching them. He glared at Olga, his eyes narrowing. "You are taking everything from me. Everything that I have spent my life building."

And as his anger grew, so did the monster inside him, stretching and lengthening until it burst forth like a snake shedding its skin. Angular wings sprouted; his neck grew and twisted. The enormous demon erupting before them was like the creatures of the forest, but without a trace of humanity remaining. Everything he had been was gone—now there was only rage and hunger. A forked tongue flicked as he gave a roar that thundered through the valley.

Olga expected him to come for her, to trample her. But instead, he turned and began to storm back toward the gardens on grotesque long legs, toppling stones, tearing branches from their boughs as his colossal form crashed past. The wings spread and he swooped low, gliding like a bird of prey toward the palace.

"He's heading for the soldiers," said Pavel.

Olga knew that she was the only one who could stop him. She was the one he had spent all these years searching for, the one he wanted.

"Stop!" she shouted, but either he was refusing to heed her, or he could no longer hear, as he continued on his rampage toward the palace.

Without thinking, Olga ran. And before long, her footsteps were joined by many others. It made her heart soar to know she was not alone.

They darted through the gardens, where hedges were trampled, bushes pulled from their roots. The stone fountain was gone. And as they approached the ballroom, the wide doors that had led from the gardens to the ballroom were now a gaping hole in the side of the palace where Baron Sokolov had crashed through.

Olga rushed toward the doors but stopped in horror at the

scene before her. The baron loomed over the crowd in his ball-room. He thrashed at the soldiers with giant wings, clawing at them with talons like sickles, knocking both humans and stones from the palace wall to the floor.

And the soldiers were readying their weapons.

"Wait!" Olga shouted, but the soldiers weren't listening—of course they weren't, when such danger gnashed its teeth at them. She had to lead the baron back outside. She darted in front of him, waving her arms. "I'm the one you want. Take my heartstring first!" she said.

She saw red eyes glowing like coals. He seemed to think for a moment, deciding. Uncertain. But then he turned, his attention once again on the soldiers, whose spears and arrows glanced off him by the dozen without leaving even a scratch.

The only thing that was going to convince him was the truth. She swallowed, her throat tight, her tongue too heavy to move. Then the truth burst from her. "I'm the one you're looking for. I'm your daughter."

And at this the creature did stop, leathery wing half raised. He blinked at her.

"It's me. I didn't know until you gave me the locket. It was my mother's portrait inside."

The creature had stopped fighting the soldiers, but still he towered over them ominously. She needed to find a way to change him back, but she'd used all the kerchiefs she'd brought. There had to be something, something that connected her and the baron.

Her mother connected them, but her mother's heartstring was gone.

And suddenly she remembered: the song that the baron had performed for his guests, the same song that Olga had heard her own mother sing as she'd fallen asleep. It was a song that he knew, a song that belonged to both of them.

"Pavel, where's your domra?" she asked.

He had it with him, and Olga had to laugh. Even on such an expedition—chasing monsters and traipsing through enchanted lakes—he had brought it. He pulled it from his pack, and Olga, not knowing whether or not this would work, took a heartstring from herself. She stretched it across the bridge of the instrument, winding it down each string and tightening the pegs.

She strummed a chord, one of the ones Pavel had taught her. And though the notes were hesitant, searching, something in the baron's giant form shifted.

"When autumn winds blow,
The songbirds all know
To spread their wings wide,
So to escape the snow."

Olga began to sing the familiar words. Memories she'd tried her best to forget resurfaced, woven through each line of the melody. They filled her with warmth and brought fresh tears to her eyes.

Love for her mother filled her, along with a pain she had tried so hard to hide.

The instrument hummed as Olga played and sang all of the heartache she had felt, and she realized that a full heart

didn't only mean one that was filled with love. She had felt fear and desperation, she had felt loneliness and sadness. But she had also felt love and joy. All of these things made her who she was. All of them made it so that she could do her own, true magic.

> *"But I shall hold strong, for*
> *No matter how long*
> *They are gone, there's a mark*
> *On my heart of their song."*

She played with her whole heart, and as she sang, the baron seemed to recognize her words, and she knew that he

understood. Slowly, his monstrous form withered, shrinking smaller and smaller until at last he was his human self once more.

Olga strummed the final note of her song, and only then did she move to approach him. He stood before her, blue eyes glistening with tears, skin and hair streaked with mud. The last musical chords still reverberated from the ballroom's stone walls. Splintered wood and debris littered the floor around her.

As she took a shaking step, an arrow appeared in the baron's chest, and he fell to his knees.

twenty-six

Olga screamed. She turned, seeing one of the soldiers with his bow still trembling. Pavel knocked the soldier to the floor, and soon others swarmed around him, grabbing his arms.

But Olga knelt at the baron's side. Though he was far more bedraggled than when Olga had first met him, he looked recognizable once more. His head had slumped against the ground, until he lifted it with effort as he gazed at her with clear eyes.

"Is it you?" he asked. He flinched with the pain of his wound. His lips were wet with blood. "Is it really you? All this time . . . you've been here and I didn't realize." His voice was heavy with regret.

Olga could say nothing.

She wanted to say that she hated what he'd become. What he'd done in his pursuit of Olga and her mother. He'd hurt the people here, hurt himself, hurt her.

Olga had once imagined that if she ever did meet her father, there would be some sort of magical connection between them, a thread tying them together. He would recognize her instantly as his daughter and swing her into an embrace. In the warmth of his arms, she would know with certainty how special he was to her and she to him.

But things weren't so simple, and he was not the perfect father she had hoped for.

He was flawed, heartbroken, desperate, cruel.

The baron's breaths had become labored, gasping. "I was a fool," he said. "I didn't see you right in front of my eyes. But at least . . ." He paused, taking a difficult breath, then reached out and touched his fingertips to her cheek. "I got to meet you. . . ."

For all his flaws, he had wanted her. Yet she was glad that her mother had decided to leave. Her mother had seen the truth inside him, that people were possessions to him, even when he believed he loved them. Thanks to her mother, and to Pavel, and now to Anna, Olga knew what love, and forgiveness, and trust truly were.

His head had become heavy. His eyes threatened to close.

Slowly, softly, she sang the familiar refrain once more.

"No matter how long
They are gone, there's a mark
On my heart of their song."

His face brightened with recognition, and he smiled.

With painful slowness, his hand moved to his chest, and he withdrew a length of his heartstring. He pressed it into her palm, closing her fingers around it.

Then he took a final shaking breath and slumped against the floor.

The soldiers had moved in as Olga knelt over the baron, but Pavel and Anna and the other guests, recently relieved of their swan bodies, had blocked the way. Spiders led by Pauk gathered around them in a protective circle.

"She saved us," said one of the guests.

"We would still be cursed without her," said another.

Magistrate Morozova stood closest, still poised with her weapon in hand. "Those monsters outside still remain."

But Olga shook her head. She knew what she had to do now to break their curse.

"I can change them," she said. "Please let me cast one last spell."

Through the gaping holes torn in the walls of the palace and its gardens, Olga could see the creatures clustered at the edge of the forest. In the blue light of early evening, their scales shimmered. Their low cry was imploring. *OooEEEaaaooo.* It carried such fear and heartache that Olga tried to inject every drop of comfort she could into her magic as she gave the domra another strum. Its chord hummed, and she sang her tune once more.

In the moonlight, the creatures shivered. They stared at each other nervously as Olga's song continued. With each word, their cursed selves drained away, scales dissolving as arms and legs sprouted. A cloud obscured the moon, and for a moment the creatures were in darkness, but as it shifted again, it was to reveal humans gathered. Olga's heart was bursting with triumph and relief. Their hair glittered in the starlight. They clasped each other and hugged and sang. Like spirits of the forest, they danced in the moonlight, letting its beams soak into their skin.

This was what her magic was meant to be, a magic that was true and honest. A magic that, when she played, she could feel coming from the valley itself.

The curse was broken.

Olga swelled with joy and relief at the distant cries of celebration. But the nearby magistrate scoffed, ignoring the recovered souls to watch Olga with distrust. "Am I to believe you've broken the spell forever? You're still a thief. Baron Sokolov described the locket you stole from him."

"Did you not hear her?" asked Mr. Bulgakov, who had appeared at the magistrate's side. "She is the baron's daughter. This is her palace. How can she steal from herself?" He gave a knowing look to Olga that she couldn't return.

Olga considered her words carefully. She was tired of wearing disguises, tired of fleeing the villagers she'd cheated. She wanted to leave her old life behind, and that meant she would no longer lie or cast an illusion to escape punishment. "If this palace is truly mine, then I want to repay those I stole from," she said to Magistrate Morozova. "Can you help me?" She held the magistrate's gaze, wishing there were some way to show that she meant what she said.

Perhaps there was, and her earnestness showed in her eyes, or her tone, or her clasped hands, because Magistrate Morozova finally nodded.

"There will be questioning so we can piece together proof of your claims of inheritance. And then I'll have a messenger deliver the names I have," she said, full of clipped words and brusque authority. "Along with what information I can find about your family."

Olga thanked her, but nearby she heard Mr. Bulgakov give a chuckle.

He waited until Magistrate Morozova had turned her attention to her soldiers to give them orders before he said to Olga in a low voice, "Well done. I almost believed you."

"I wasn't lying," said Olga. "Not everything is a trick. Unless it's coming from you. You brought these soldiers here." She was unable to hide the accusation from her words.

Mr. Bulgakov wasn't at all taken aback by her tone, and Olga recognized the cool and collected voice he used when bargaining. "Morozova had men follow us all the way from that last village. They were going to take me into custody until I explained that if they ventured into this valley"—he paused, and there was a sly twinkle in his eye—"then they could have a share in any treasure you might have found."

"And they trusted you?" Olga said.

He merely winked. "Money holds as much sway with them as with anyone," he said. "Remember, there's always a third option in a bargain."

He waited for her reply, as if this were a new lesson she should accept with gratitude. But Olga found that she didn't want to hear his advice anymore.

"They could have been killed." The thought made her shiver a little. It seemed all too similar to something the baron would have done.

"And the treasure would be entirely ours if they were."

Olga couldn't respond. She didn't want to argue with him about treasure, or jewels, or who owned what. The wounds were still too raw.

Instead, she left him standing in the middle of the ballroom as she sought the rest of her friends.

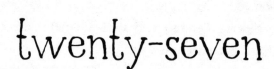

twenty-seven

In the gardens, the spiders were gathering. Mokosh stood amongst them, covered in hundreds of her loyal subjects. As Olga approached, she could see that the spider queen had begun to shift, her human features slipping away. She was returning to a form more wholly spider, one of the great beings who protected the valley.

"I'm ready to rest again," Mokosh said, her lips twitching. "But you have the support of my subjects, if ever you need to ask." A small cluster of spiders on her arm dipped their legs in a bow.

Olga clasped that hand, careful not to crush the spiders on her wrist. "Thank you. For the magic. For helping me find it."

Mokosh gave a low chuckle as she said, "Just don't do anything that will wake me again. I am very tired." Yet there was a spark in her voice as she added, "Thank you for letting me do some final spinning. I have faith in the future, having met you."

In her chest, Olga's heartstring warmed and hummed, not with power but with gratitude. She vowed to use it from now on as it was always meant to be: a gift worth treasuring, from the heart.

The spider queen's subjects were tugging at her gown, ready to lead her toward the gate, to her forest home. Olga's heart pounded as she realized this was their farewell, and she wasn't ready. She owed so much to Mokosh—for her magic, yes, but also for what Olga had found here in the valley. For her family, her past and future. How could she offer a gift that would express what was in her heart?

Her hand clenched, and she realized she was still grasping her father's heartstring. She held it out, the meager thread a dull shimmer on her palms. "Please take it," she said.

Mokosh observed the heartstring, her expression a mix of gravity and anticipation. "Are you sure?" she asked.

Olga was.

With skeletal fingers, the spider queen plucked the strand. She turned and pressed the string to the ground near a forlorn rosebush. As she wrapped it around its base, the flowers blossomed, their scent filling the air. Delicate yellow and orange petals unfolded, the color of a sunrise.

"Now it can grow into something beautiful," Mokosh said.

It seemed perfect, something connected to what he'd loved, something real. The heartstring wasn't the end of this story, it was the beginning of a new one.

When Olga looked up to thank Mokosh, she found that the spider queen was gone. But she thought she heard the

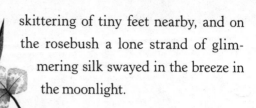

skittering of tiny feet nearby, and on the rosebush a lone strand of glimmering silk swayed in the breeze in the moonlight.

When morning dawned, and the soldiers departed from the palace, Olga decided to tell Mr. Bulgakov that it was time for him to depart too. She would be sorry to see him go, though not sorry enough to consider joining him. She was grateful that he had kept her fed and sheltered all these years, and he had cared for her in his own rough way. But Olga needed to find her own path, and it would begin with her staying in the palace.

He took the news about as well as could be expected.

"Keeping the Scarlet Heart for yourself, are you?" he asked with a slight sneer.

But the harsh words didn't sting, because she knew there was no truth to them. "It doesn't exist. At least, it's not a real jewel," she tried to explain.

He nodded, though she could tell he didn't believe her. It wasn't surprising—after so many years of telling lies.

"And what will you do, Olga?" he asked, and Olga was

reminded of a time when he'd asked a similar question not so long ago. He sounded surprisingly thoughtful, perhaps a hint of concern peeking through after all.

Olga shrugged and smiled. She wasn't sure what she would choose to do next, but she did know one thing: she wanted Pavel and Anna beside her.

Pavel helped to ready the cart while Anna fed and brushed Fabiy and secured his harness. Smiles of love and contentment lit their faces. Pavel planted a kiss on Anna's cheek, then came to stand beside Olga. His heavy hand landed on Olga's shoulder, and the force of his strength nearly knocked her to her knees.

Together they bade their old guardian farewell, their

emotions mixed, undefinable. Olga wished the best for him, but not at the expense of those he'd try to swindle.

Mr. Bulgakov gave a final glance toward the turrets and windows, and he shivered. He still saw the palace as somewhere sinister, and Olga couldn't blame him. Now, this place was filled with cobwebs and haunted memories. But thanks to Pavel and Anna and Mokosh, she could imagine what it might become: a place to share a warm meal together, and laughter, and maybe even a song by the fireside. And when wanderers came to the valley in search of truth or beauty or the cure for a broken heart, all would be welcome.

"Good luck," Mr. Bulgakov said, though he sounded doubtful. He touched a hand to his cap and flicked Fabiy's reins. The cart rattled up the road and disappeared between the trees.

Not until days later would Olga notice missing the candlesticks he'd taken with him.

Like Mr. Bulgakov, many of the former swans left the valley in the following days, returning to their home villages. Some of them left the Kamen Mountains for towns elsewhere in the tsardom. Others asked to stay in the palace, for they had no homes to return to. Olga was glad to have them, as were Pavel and Anna. The trio had begun to clean the wreckage the baron's rampage had left behind, and to repair what remained in the palace now that the collapse of his illusions revealed how much of it had fallen into ruin during the years under his curse.

Anna already had grand hopes for the restoration, and her words painted a dreamy portrait of a place with delicate spiderweb canopies and jeweled birds gracing the surrounding forest. Pauk seemed on board with the idea, and he had already begun recruiting other spiders to assist in the decorating. Pavel's first focus was to free the birds in the aviary, then to dust and repair the instruments. He was still drawn to the fashionable clothes and fine fabrics. Olga and Anna even helped with mending and alterations when needed.

Olga heard their proposals with pleasure. For the first time in her memory, she didn't have a plan, and she wanted to enjoy that feeling for a moment. Soon the time would come when her new future would take shape. Soon. But for now, she was happy to let their schemes and dreams guide her.

Always, the halls rang with the sound of Pavel's domra. Olga and Anna would lend their voices to his, clapping and jumping as they sang.

"Wherever you are, I am home.
Together we're never alone."

The palace would never be as glamorous as it had been under her father's enchantments, but it was real, and so was the love within it.

There would be stories, of course, of people who had long

been missing, returning as if from the grave. And those stories would have some truth to them, though many would be embellished, filled with frightful tales of witches and monsters passed on from person to person until they were no longer recognizable.

But they started in truth. And Olga couldn't help but grin with each happily ever after.

"I will not tell you the rest, little ones,"
said the spider. "It is up to you
to take the strand and decide
where it may lead."

Author's Note

The origins of the story of *Swan Lake* are somewhat mysterious, which seems appropriate for such a tale. It bears similarities to different versions of the "Swan Maiden" fairy-tale structure found in stories such as *The Stolen Veil* and *The White Duck*. Neither of those stories align exactly with the plot of *Swan Lake*, and while it contains elements from both of them, it seems to be an original tale. The story also changed significantly as the ballet took shape, with an originally tragic ending shifting to one of hope over several iterations between the 1870s and the 1890s.

In my own research into the story, I was curious to understand its origins. Though the music was written by a Russian composer, the characters' names—Odette, Prince Siegfried, Baron von Rothbart—are French and German. There is some speculation that the story was influenced by the untimely death of King Ludwig II of Bavaria (who was sometimes referred to as the "Swan King" due to his coat of arms). I ultimately decided to give the story a Slavic-inspired setting in an original world, giving the characters names of the original/early dancers, with the exception of Mokosh, who is a goddess from Slavic mythology known for her spinning and weaving and is sometimes connected with spiders.

In keeping with that setting, I took inspiration from two similar but distinct creatures from Slavic folklore:

Rusalki, often translated into English as meaning "mermaids," are demons said to haunt bodies of water. They are sometimes thought to be the spirits of women who died by drowning. Beautiful, with long hair, they lure men to watery deaths, similar to sirens in other mythologies. Early drafts of this book cast the baron as a woman, a spirit who had drowned in the lake.

Vili (wili, samodivi, among other names and spellings) are also the ghostly spirits of jilted women who lure men to their deaths; however, they usually haunt forests and capture people by dancing. The ballet *Giselle* depicts a group of "wilis" who attempt to lure a nobleman to his death before he is saved by the "wili" Giselle, who still loves him. Vili can take the form of animals (including swans, but also wolves, falcons, and horses) by donning magic cloaks. It is said that a vila can be defeated if one steals or burns the animal cloak she keeps hidden while she is in human form.

Giselle and *Swan Lake* are two of my favorite ballets, and while I have taken liberties with both their stories and the folklore informing them, I hope this book can be read as a loving tribute.

Acknowledgments

I am grateful to those who helped this book throughout its long, pandemic-addled process. Ralph, thank you for everything. Your humor, your creative insight, your encouragement, your love. Katie Grimm, my agent, who I am very lucky to partner with on this publishing journey. Katherine Harrison, my editor, who saw the heart of this book and pushed it to be its best self. Pauliina Hannuniemi, Bob Bianchini, and Jen Valero for illustrations and design beyond my wildest dreams.

At Knopf Books for Young Readers and Random House Children's Books, thank you to Gianna Lakenauth, Artie Bennett, Renée Cafiero, Lisa Leventer, Lili Feinberg, Kathy Dunn, Nathan Kinney, Jake Eldred, and so many more for your work on this book and A Wolf for a Spell.

Lots of writers read iterations of this book, and I especially appreciate those who suffered through terrible early drafts and still gave words of encouragement. Adrianna Cuevas, Swati Teerdhala, Scott Rhoades, Adelle Yeung, Jennifer Lauren Brown, Diana DeBolt Johnson, and thanks to Graci Kim and Mel Harding-Shaw for the chats and support. Kathy, Claire, Lauren, Sarah: all the love and hugs. And love and thank you to my talented creative whānau in Aotearoa and Australia: Jeremy, Maddi, Joel, Mouce, Zola, Claire, Marcus, Saoirse, Fiona, Julian, Caspian, Nicola, and Polly. To my PikPok team, who asked me to sign their books and sent words of encouragement on my writing days. And to Amanda, Cheryl, Evan, and other former bookstore colleagues who have been such champions.

I wouldn't be who I am without my family. To Mom, Maia, Sabrina, Matt, and Dad: I love you. And love and thanks to the Uptons, Norrisses, and Mendells: especially with this book to Philippa for reading and sharing thoughtful insights, to fellow writers Jeanette and Greg for their passionate support, and to Ravi, Charlie, Imogen, Harriet, Henry, Sebastian, and Zoe.

To anyone who read and shared *A Wolf for a Spell*, thank you. This book is for you.

About the Author

Karah Sutton is an American/New Zealand children's author and former bookseller. Her debut middle-grade fantasy adventure, *A Wolf for a Spell,* was an American Booksellers Association Indies Introduce selection, an Indie Next List Top 10 selection, and a Junior Library Guild selection and was nominated for a Goodreads Choice Award. Inspired by her many years as a ballet dancer, *The Song of the Swan* is her second novel. Karah spins her stories in a house by the sea in New Zealand.

KarahSutton.com